MR J. G. REEDER RETURNS

Mr J. G. Reeder Returns

by

Edgar Wallace

Dales Large Print Books
Long Preston, North Yorkshire,
BD23 4ND, England.

British Library Cataloguing in Publication Data.

Wallace, Edgar
   Mr J. G. Reeder Returns.

   A catalogue record of this book is
   available from the British Library

   ISBN   1-84262-314-1 pbk

Published in Large Print 2004 by arrangement with
House of Stratus

Dales Large Print is an imprint of Library Magna Books Ltd.

Printed and bound in Great Britain by
T.J. (International) Ltd., Cornwall, PL28 8RW

THE TREASURE HOUSE

1

Mr J.G Reeder did odd things. And he did oddly kind things. There was once a drug addict, whom he first prosecuted and then befriended; but there was nothing unusual in that. He did the same with a young man many years later, and as a result earned for himself the high commendation of his superiors.

But helping this drug addict led apparently nowhere. It involved a great deal of trouble, and it was an unsavoury case, and in the end Mr Reeder achieved nothing, for the man he tried to assist died in hospital without friends and without money.

It is true that the man in the next bed knew him, and communicated a great deal of information to a ferret-faced chauffeur, who subsequently made certain inquiries.

A more satisfactory adventure in the field of loving kindness was Mr Reeder's association with a certain well-educated young

9

burglar. That led to much that was pleasant to think about and remember.

The story of the treasure house really begins with a man who had no faith in the stability of stock markets, and believed in burying his talents in the ground. He was not singular in this respect, for the miser in man is a very common quality, and though Mr Lane Leonard was no miser in the strictest sense of the word, being in fact rather generous of disposition, he was wedded to the reality of wealth, and there is nothing quite so real as gold. And gold he accumulated in startling quantities at a period when gold was hard to come by. Gold in buried chests would not satisfy him; he must have gold visible and reachable – but mainly visible. That is why he hoarded his wealth in large boxes made of toughened glass, having these containers further enclosed in steel wire baskets; for gold is very heavy and the toughest of glass is brittle.

They said on the New York Stock Exchange that John Lane Leonard was a lucky man, but he never regarded himself that way. He was not a member of the house, and had begun as a dabbler in the kerb market, buying on margins and accumulating a very modest fortune, which became colossal overnight, through no prescience of his own, but rather because of a lucky accident. He was as near to being ruined as made no difference. Three partners, who had pooled their shares with him, became panic stricken at a bear raid and left him to hold the baby; and whilst he was holding this very helplessly, not quite sure whether he should drop it and run, powerful financial interests, of whose existence he was quite unaware, struck so savagely at the bears that they were caught short. The sensational rise in prices placed Mr Lane Leonard rich in excess of his own imagination.

He was not a millionaire then, but he had not long to wait before another piece of luck brought him into the seven-figure class. If he had had a sense of humour, he would have recognised just how much he owed to the spin of somebody else's coin; but, being devoid of this quality, he gave large credit to his own acumen and foresight. There were any number of people who fostered the illusion that he had the mind and vision of a great financier. His brother-in-law, Digby Olbude, was one of his most vehement and voluble sycophants.

Lane Leonard was English, and had married an English wife; a dull lady, who hated New York and was homesick for Hampstead, a pleasant suburb it was designed she should never see again. She died, more or less of inanition, three years after her husband had acquired both his riches and a sneaking desire for American citizenship.

By this time John Lane Leonard was an authority on all matters pertaining to finance. He wrote articles for the *London Economist* which were never published, because in some way they did not fit in with the views of the editor, or, indeed, with the views of anybody who had an elementary knowledge of economics. Whatever Digby thought about them, he said they were great. He used to drink in those days and dabble in margins and when he lost, as he so frequently did, John Lane Leonard paid.

They parted at last over a matter of a hundred thousand dollars, and although this sum also had to be found by the millionaire, it was in his heart to forgive his erratic relative by marriage, for he never forgot that Digby completely approved of and admired him, and had helped him considerably in his preparation of a pamphlet on the American Economy. That pamphlet was so scarified by the American press, so ridiculed by the experts of Wall Street, that Mr Lane Leonard shook the dust of New York from his feet, transferred his bank balances to England, returned to his native Kent and bought Sevenways Castle and proceeded to put his theories into practice.

He met a pretty widow with a young child and married her. Within a few years she too had died. He changed the name of her little daughter by deed poll from Pamela Dolby to Pamela Lane Leonard, and designated her his heiress. It was necessary that he should have an heiress, though he would have preferred an heir.

In those days Lidgett was his junior chauffeur, a hatchet-faced boy, country born, shrewd, cunning, ruthless; but Mr Lane Leonard knew nothing about his cunning or ruthlessness. He received from Lidgett a wholehearted homage which was very pleasing to him. Lidgett did not prostrate himself on the ground every time he saw his employer – he just stopped short of that. He became the confidential servant and valet as well as chief chauffeur. Mr Lane Leonard used to talk to him about the gold standard whilst he was dressing, and Lidgett used to shake his head in helpless admiration.

'What a brain you must have, Mr Leonard! It beats me how you can keep these things in your mind! If I knew as much as you, I think I'd go mad!'

Crude stuff, but crude stuff is effective. To Lidgett Mr Lane Leonard revealed his great plan for the creation of a gold reserve; it took three weeks for Lidgett to realise that his employer was talking about real gold. After that he became very alert.

Mr Leonard was an assiduous churchgoer, and invariably chose Evensong for his devotions. When they were in London Lidgett used to sit at the wheel of the Rolls parked outside St George's, Hanover Square, wildly cursing the employer who was keeping him from a perfect evening's entertainment. There was a spieling club in Soho which was a second home to Mr Lidgett, and as soon as his master was indoors and made comfortable for the night, Lidgett lost no time in reaching the green table where they played *chemin de fer.*

His employer was a careless man, who never missed a five-pound note one way or the other, and Lidgett was a lucky man at the table, more lucky than the dignified and middle-aged gentleman he so often met at Dutch Harry's, and who seemed to come there only to lose.

Once he borrowed twenty pounds from Lidgett and found some difficulty in repaying it. Joe Lidgett got to know all about him; rather liked him, if the truth be told.

'You ought to give up this game, mister. You haven't got the right kind of nut.'

'Very possible, very possible,' said the other frigidly.

Sometimes in the early hours of the morning the little Cockney and his somewhat aristocratic friend would go to an all-night restaurant for a meal before they separated, the unfortunate loser to an early train which carried him into the country, Mr Lidgett to his duties as chauffeur-valet.

In the course of his confidences with Lidgett Mr Leonard mentioned his brother-in-law, and enlarged upon his genius.

'He is one of the few men who really understand my theories, Lidgett,' he said in an expansive moment. 'Unfortunately, he and I quarrelled over a trifling matter, and I haven't heard from him for many years. A sound financier, Lidgett, a very sound financier! I have been tempted lately to get in touch with him; he is the one man I could trust to carry out my wishes if what this infernal doctor says has any foundation in fact.'

'This infernal doctor' was a Harley Street specialist who had said something rather serious; or it would have been serious if Mr Leonard had regarded himself as being completely mortal.

He saw little of his stepdaughter. She was at a school, came home for dull holidays, and listened uncomprehendingly to Mr Leonard's lectures on gold values. She saw the first treasure house built, inspected its steel doors, and thought that the vault was a little terrifying; she heard that all this was for her sake, but could never quite believe that.

One day Mr Leonard had a fainting fit which lasted for an hour. When he recovered he sent for Lidgett.

'Lidgett, I want you to get in touch with Mr Digby Olbude,' he said. 'I haven't his address, but you will probably find it in the telephone book. I have never troubled to look.'

He explained just what he wanted of Mr Olbude and Lidgett listened with interest, his agile mind working with great rapidity. Digby Olbude was to carry on the work of his brother-in-law, was to become for a number of years controller of untold wealth.

Lidgett went forth on his tour of investigation, wondering in what manner he might benefit from the change which most evidently was due.

Digby Olbude was not difficult to trace, though he seemed to have changed his name on two occasions and at his last address had no name at all. The shrewd little chauffeur came back to Sevenways, a very preoccupied man. He found awaiting him a letter forwarded from London – a pathetic, pleading, incoherent letter, written in perfect English by his middle-aged gambler friend.

Joe Lidgett had an idea. A few days later his master was well enough to see him and he gave an account of his search for Digby Olbude.

'I would like to see him,' said Leonard feebly. 'I am afraid I'm in a bad way, Lidgett – where are you?'

'I'm here, sir,' said Lidgett.

'It is rather difficult to see. My eyesight has become a little defective.'

The gentleman Mr Lidgett had found arrived by car the next morning. He went up more than a little nervously to the dying man's bedroom, and was introduced with pathetic formality to the lawyer Mr Leonard had brought from London. He did not like lawyers, but the occasion demanded expert legal assistance.

'This is my brother-in-law, Digby Olbude...'

The will was signed and witnessed with some difficulty. It was characteristic of Lane Leonard that he did not even send for his heiress or leave any message of affection or tender farewell. To him she was a peg on which his theory was to hang – and it was not even his own theory.

She was notified of his passing in a formal letter from her new guardian, and she received the notification on the very day that Larry O'Ryan decided upon adopting a criminal career.

When Larry O'Ryan was expelled from a public school on a charge of stealing some eighty-five pounds from Mr Farthingale's room, he could not only have cleared himself of the accusation, but he could also have named the culprit.

He had no parents, no friends, being maintained at the school by a small annuity left by his mother. If Creed's Bank had been a little more generous with his father, if the Panton Credit Trust had been honestly directed, if the Medway and Western had not forced a sale, Larry would have been rich.

It was no coincidence that these immensely rich corporations were patrons of the Monarch Security Steel Corporation – Monarchs had a monopoly in this kind of work – but we will talk about that later.

He hated the school, hated most the pompous pedagogue who was a friend of Mr Farthingale and used his study when the housemaster was out – but he said nothing. After all, what chance had his word against a master's? He took his expulsion as an easy way of escaping from servitude, interviewed the lawyer who was his guardian and accepted the expressions of horror and abhorrence with which that gentleman favoured him.

Anyway, the eighty-five pounds was restored; before he left the school Larry saw the terrified thief and said a few plain words.

'I'll take the risk of being disbelieved,' he said, 'and I'll go to the head and say I saw you open the cash-box just as I was going into the study. I don't know why you wanted the money, but the people who investigate will find out.'

The accused man thundered at him, reviled him, finally broke.

It was a grotesque situation, a middle-aged master and lanky sixth-form boy, bullying and threatening one another alternately. Larry did not cry; on the other hand, his protagonist grew maudlin. But he restored the money. Everybody thought that it was Larry or Larry's lawyer-guardian who sent the notes by registered post; but it wasn't.

He went out into the world with the starkest outlook, looked round for work of sorts, was errand boy, office boy, clerk. No prospects. The army offered one, but the army stood for another kind of school discipline, housemasters who wore stripes on their sleeves.

2

Larry thought it over one Saturday night and decided on burglary as a profession. For a year he went to night classes and polished up his knowledge of ballistics. At the end of the year he got a job at a safe-makers and locksmith's at Wolverhampton.

It was one of the most famous of all safe-makers, a firm world-renowned. All that a young man could learn of locks and safety devices Larry learned. He was an eager pupil; having a pleasant and engaging manner, he made friends with oldish men who, in return for the respect he paid them, told him many things about locks and safe construction.

He became an expert cutter of keys – had the use of a shed in the backyard of the widow with whom he lodged, and worked far into the night.

A gymnasium attached to a boys' club lent strength to skill.

When he left Wolverhampton his successes were startling and, in a newspaper sense, sensational. Creed's Bank lost forty thousand pounds in American currency held to liquidate certain demands which were due. Nobody saw the burglar come or go. The steel doors of the vault were opened with a key and locked with a key.

Then the Panton Credit Trust suffered. A matter of a hundred thousand pounds went in less than a hundred and twenty minutes.

At his third job he fell, due largely to the precautions taken on behalf of the Medway and Western Bank by a middle-aged detective who read the lessons of the earlier robberies aright; and had discovered that other banks had vault doors recently delivered and erected by the Monarch Safe Corporation.

Inquiries made at the works identified the enthusiastic young workman with a young gentleman who lived in a Jermyn Street flat and who had an account at the bank.

'It was,' said Mr Reeder apologetically, 'more by – um – luck than judgement that I succeeded in – er – anticipating this young man.'

He liked Larry from the first interview he had with him, and that was in a cell at Bow Street. Larry was quite unlike any of the criminals with whom Mr Reeder had been brought into contact. He neither whined nor lied, neither boasted nor was evasive. Mr Reeder did not know his history and was unable to trace it.

'It's a great pity you're so clever, Mr Reeder. This was to have been my final appearance as a burglar – hereafter I intended living the life of a well-to-do citizen, and hoped in course of time to become a Justice of the Peace!'

Mr Reeder rarely smiled, but he did now.

'The other incursions into the burglar's profession were, I presume – um – Creed's Bank and the Panton Trust?'

It was Larry's turn to smile.

'That is a matter we will not discuss,' he said politely.

Mr Reeder, however, was more anxious to keep the matter in discussion, for there was a sum of a hundred and forty thousand pounds to be recovered.

'You will be ill-advised, Mr O'Ryan,' he said gently, 'to withhold these very important facts, particularly the whereabouts of – um – a very considerable sum which was taken from these two institutions. A complete disclosure will make a very considerable difference to you when you – er – come before the judge. I do not promise this,' he

23

added carefully; 'I am merely going on precedents, but it is a fact that judges, in passing sentence, take into consideration the frankness with which an – um – accused person has dealt with his earlier depredations.'

Larry O'Ryan laughed softly.

'That's a lovely word – depredations! It also makes me feel like one of the old robber barons of the Rhine. No, Mr Reeder – nicely but firmly, no! In the first place, the two – depredations was the word, I think, you used? – to which you refer, are not and cannot be traceable to me. I have read about them and I know the facts which have been revealed in the newspapers. Beyond that I am not prepared to admit the slightest knowledge.'

J.G Reeder was insistent in his amiable way. He revealed his own information. He knew that O'Ryan had been employed by the Monarch Security Steel Corporation, he knew that it was possible he might have secured an understanding of the locks which had been so scientifically defied; and since all three institutions had obtained their steel vaults, their unbreakable doors, their gratings and secret locking arrangements from this company, there was no doubt in his mind (he said) that O'Ryan was responsible for both burglaries. But Larry shook his head.

'The burden of proof lies with the prosecution,' he said with mock solemnity. 'I should like very much indeed to help you, Mr Reeder. I have heard of you, I admire you. Any man who in these days wears high-crowned felt hats and side-whiskers must have character, and I admire character. I hope that reference is not offensive to you; it is intended to be nothing but complimentary. I know quite a lot about you. You live in the Brockley Road, you keep chickens, you have an umbrella which you never open for fear it will be spoilt by the rain, and you smoke unspeakable cigarettes.'

Again that rare smile of Mr Reeder's.

'You're almost a detective,' he said. 'Now, let us talk about Creed's Bank—'

'Let us talk about the weather,' said Larry.

All Scotland Yard, and the Public Prosecutor's Department, and Mr Reeder, and various narks and noses, and the parasites of the underworld were concerned in the search for the missing hundred and forty thousand pounds, even though there was not sufficient evidence to indict Larry for these two crimes.

In due course he appeared before a judge at the Old Bailey, and pleaded guilty to being found on enclosed premises in possession of burglar's tools, and to housebreaking (he had entered the bank at four o'clock on a Saturday afternoon) and, after a rather acrimonious trial, was found guilty and sentenced to a term of twelve months in prison.

The trial was acrimonious because the counsel for the prosecution took a personal and violent dislike to the prisoner. Why, nobody knew; it was one of those prejudices which occasionally upset the judgement of intelligent men. It was probably some flippant remark which Larry made in cross-examination, a remark which counsel regarded as personally offensive to himself. He was not a big man, and he was rather a self-willed man. In his address to the jury he referred to the Creed's Bank robbery and the burglary at the Panton Trust. At the first reference to these affairs the judge stopped and warned him, but he was not to be warned. Although no evidence had been called, and no charge made, in relation to these crimes, he insisted upon drawing parallels. He emphasised the fact that the prisoner had been employed by the company which made the locks and steel doors of both vaults; and all the time Larry sat in the dock, his arms folded, listening with a smile, for he knew something about law. ℯ

There was an appeal; the conviction was quashed on a technical point, and Larry O'Ryan went free.

His first call was on Mr J.G Reeder, and he prefaced his visit with a short note asking whether his presence was acceptable. Reeder asked him to tea, which was the equivalent of being asked by the Lord Mayor to his most important banquet. Larry came in the highest spirits.

'May I say,' asked Mr Reeder, 'that you are a very fortunate young man?'

'And how!' said Larry. 'Yes, I was lucky. But who would imagine that the idiot would make a mistake like that! Are you sure you don't mind my calling?'

Mr Reeder shook his head.

'If you hadn't come I should have invited you,' he said.

With a pair of silver tongs he placed a muffin on Larry's plate.

'It would be a waste of time, Mr O'Ryan, and I rather think a breach of – um – hospitality, if I made any further reference to those other unfortunate happenings, the

– um – Creed's Bank and Panton Trust affairs. As a detective and an officer of state, I should be most happy if I could find one little string of a clue which would enable me to associate you with those – um – depredations is the word, I think, you like best?'

'Depredations is my favourite word,' mumbled Larry through the muffin.

'Somehow, I don't think I shall ever be able to connect you,' Mr Reeder went on, 'and in a sense I'm rather glad. That is a very immoral statement to make,' he added hastily, 'and against all my – um – principles, as you probably know. What are you going to do for a living now, Mr O'Ryan?'

'I am living on my income,' said Larry calmly. 'I have investments aboard which will bring me in, roughly, seven thousand a year.'

Mr Reeder nodded slowly.

'In other words, five per cent on a hundred and forty thousand pounds,' he murmured. 'A goodly sum – a very goodly sum.' He sighed.

'You don't seem very happy about it.' Larry's eyes twinkled.

Mr Reeder shook his head.

'No, I am thinking of the poor shareholders

of Creed's Bank–'

'There are no shareholders. The Creeds practically hold the shares between them. They tricked my father out of a hundred thousand pounds – a little more than that sum. I have never had the full particulars, but I know it was a hundred thousand – snapped it out of his pocket, and there was no possibility of getting back on them.'

J.G looked at the ceiling.

'So it was an act of poetic justice!' he said slowly. 'And Panton Trust?'

'You know the Panton crowd,' said Larry quietly. 'They have been living on the edge of highway robbery for the past twenty-five years. They've made most of their money out of crooked companies and tricky share dealing. They owe me much more than – they lost.'

A beatific smile passed over Mr Reeder's face.

'You nearly said, "than I took,"' he said reproachfully.

'I nearly didn't say anything of the kind,' said Larry. 'No, don't waste your sympathy on them. And I could tell you something about the Medway and Western Bank that would interest you, but I won't.'

'Poetic justice again, eh? You are almost a

romantic figure!'

Mr Reeder grasped the teapot and refilled the young man's cup.

'I'll promise you something; we'll not discuss this matter again, but I'll be very glad to see you any time you find life a little wearisome and would like to discover how really dull it can be. At the same time, I feel I should – um – warn you that if you – er – fall from grace and desire to wreak your poetic vengeance upon some other banking institution, these little visits will cease, and I shall do my best to put you behind locks which were not manufactured by the Monarch Security Steel Corporation!'

Larry became a fairly frequent visitor to the house in Brockley Road. Some people might have suspected Mr Reeder of maintaining the acquaintance in order to secure further information about the earlier robberies. But Larry did not suspect Mr Reeder of anything of the sort, and J.G appreciated this compliment more than the young man knew.

Larry got into the habit of calling at night, and particularly when an interesting crime had been committed. He knew very little of the so-called underworld, and surprised Mr Reeder when he told him that he had never met a crook until he was arrested.

This oddly matched pair had another interest in common; the British Museum. A visit to the museum was Larry's favourite recreation. Mr Reeder, whenever he could find the time, invariably spent his Saturday afternoons in its heavily instructive atmosphere. And they both found their interest in the same psychology. Mr Reeder loved to stand before the Elgin marbles and picture the studio in old Greece where these figures grew under the chisel of the master. He would stand for hours, looking down at a mummy, reconstructing the living woman who lay swathed behind the bandages. What was her life, her interests, her friends? How did she amuse herself? Had she children? What were they called? Did she find life boring or amusing? Did she have trouble with her servants?

Larry's mind ran in the same direction. They would stand before some ancient missal and conjure up a picture of the tonsured monk who worked in his cell, illuminating and writing with great labour the black lettering which was there under their eyes. When he opened the cell door and walked out into the world, what kind of a world was it? To whom did he speak?

Sometimes they varied their Saturday afternoons by a visit to the Tower. Who put that stone upon the other? What was his name? Where did he live? In what hovel? Who were his friends? A Norman artisan, brought by William across the seas. Possibly his name was Pierre, Mr Reeder would hazard after a long, long silence.

'Gaston,' suggested Larry.

Only once did they even speak of Larry's grisly past. It was an evening which they spent together in town. Mr Reeder had just completed the evidence in the Central Bank robbery and was weary. They were dining in a little restaurant in Soho, when Larry asked: 'Do you know anything about the Lane Leonard estate?'

Mr Reeder took off his glasses, polished them, put them on again and allowed them to sag and drop.

'Before I answer that question will you be good enough to tell me what you mean by that inquiry?'

Larry grinned.

'There's no need to be cautious. I'll tell you what brought the subject up – that iron grille before the cashier's desk. It's almost the same pattern as one we made for the Lane Leonard estate. I suppose they've got trust deeds to guard. They've certainly got one of the strongest steel vaults that's ever been supplied to a corporation that wasn't a bank.'

Mr Reeder beckoned a waiter and ordered coffee.

'The Lane Leonard estate is presumably the estate of the late John Lane Leonard. He was a millionaire who died three years ago, leaving an immense fortune to his stepdaughter – I forget the exact amount, but it was somewhere between one and two million pounds.'

'He wasn't a banker?' asked Larry curiously.

Mr Reeder shook his head.

'No, he was not a banker. So far as I know, he was an American stockbroker, who was a very heavy speculator in shares, a man who had the intelligence to keep the money he had won on the Stock Exchange. He had a vault made, you say?'

Larry nodded.

'The strongest I've ever seen. Not large, but triple steel-plated walls and two doors, and all the tricks and safeguards that money could buy. I looked it over when it was completed, and I had a talk with the men who assembled it.'

He thought for a moment.

'That must have been just before he died. It was just over three years ago. He must have had some pretty hefty securities, but why shouldn't they be kept at the bank?'

Mr Reeder looked at him reproachfully.

'There are many reasons why securities should not be kept at the bank,' he said, 'and you are – er – one of them.'

Mr Reeder thought of the Lane Leonard estate on his way back to Brockley. Unusual happenings fascinated him. He tried to recall the particulars of the Lane Leonard will. He had read it at the time, but he could not recall that there was anything remarkable about it.

When he got home he looked up a work of reference. Miss Lane Leonard, the heiress, lived at Sevenways Castle, in Kent; Sevenways being a little village in the Isle of Thanet. He could recollect nothing about the family which was in any way interesting, or that had interested him. He had never seen the place, for duty had not brought him into the neighbourhood; but he remembered dimly having seen a photograph of an imposing mansion, and had a faint idea that at some time it had been a royal property, that of the seventh or eighth Henry.

3

It was shortly after this little talk that J.G Reeder made the acquaintance of Mr Buckingham. It was made in a public place, to Mr Reeder's embarrassment, for he hated publicity. On that same day he had had an exchange of words with the Assistant Public Prosecutor. That official had sent for him and was a little embarrassed.

'I don't want to bother you, Mr Reeder,' he said, 'particularly as I know you have your own peculiar method of working. But a report has come to this office that you have been seen very frequently in the company of the man who was charged at the Old Bailey and whose sentence was quashed on appeal. I think you ought to know this. I have told those concerned that you are probably trying to get information about the other two robberies. I suppose I am right in this?'

'No, sir,' said Mr Reeder, 'you are most emphatically not right.'

When Mr Reeder was definite he was very definite. 'I am not even trying to keep this young man to the path of rectitude. A detective, sir, is like a journalist; he may be seen in any company without losing caste. I like Mr O'Ryan; he is very interesting, and I shall see him just as often as I wish to see him, and if the department – um – feels that I am acting in any way derogatory to its dignity, or impairing its authority, I am prepared to place my resignation in its hands forthwith.'

This was a Reeder which the Assistant Prosecutor did not know, but of which he had heard – Mr Reeder the imperious, the dictatorial. It was not a pleasant experience.

'There is no reason why you should take that tone, Mr Reeder–' he began.

'That is the tone I invariably employ with any person or persons who interfere in the slightest degree with my private life,' said Mr Reeder.

The Assistant Prosecutor telephoned his chief, who was in the country, and the Public Prosecutor replied very tersely and to the point.

'Let him do as he wishes. For God's sake don't interfere with him!' he said testily. 'Reeder is quite capable of looking after himself and his own reputation.'

So Mr Reeder went in a sort of mild

triumph to the Queen's Hall, where Larry was waiting for him, and together they sat and listened to a classical programme which was wholly incomprehensible to J.G Reeder, but which he suffered rather than offend his companion.

'Wonderful!' breathed Larry, as the last trembling notes of a violin were engulfed in a thunder of applause.

'Extraordinary,' agreed Mr Reeder. 'I didn't recognise the tune, but he seemed to play the fiddle rather nicely.'

'You're a Philistine, Mr Reeder,' groaned Larry.

Mr Reeder shook his head sadly.

'I'm afraid I shall never be able to appreciate these peculiar sounds which – um – so interest you,' he said. 'I have a liking for old songs; in fact, I think "In the Gloaming" is one of the most beautiful pieces I have ever heard–'

'Come and have a drink,' said Larry, in despair.

This was during the interval, and they made their way to the bar at the back of the stalls. It was here that Mr Buckingham made his dramatic entrance.

He was a tall, broad-shouldered man, red of face, rough of speech; his hair was unruly, his eyes a little wild, and he moved in a nidor of spirituous liquor. He stared glassily at Mr Reeder, reached out a big and ugly hand.

'You're Mr Reeder, ain't you?' he said thickly. 'I've been thinking of coming to see you, and I would have come, only I've been busy. Fancy meeting you here! I've seen you often in court.'

Mr Reeder took the hand and dropped it. He hated moist hands. So far as he could recall, he had never met the man before, but evidently he was known to him. As though he read his thoughts, the other went on:

'My name's Buckingham. I used to be in 'L' Division.' Leaning forward, he asked confidentially, 'Have you ever heard such muck?'

Evidently this disrespectful reference was to the concert.

'I wouldn't have come, but my girlfriend made me. She's highbrow!' He winked. 'I'll introduce her.'

He dived into the crowd and returned, dragging a pallid-looking girl with a long, unhealthy face, who was not so highbrow that she despised the source of Mr Buckingham's inspiration, for her eyes too were a little glassy.

38

'One of these days I'll come and talk to you,' said Buckingham. 'I don't know whether I'll have to, but I may have to; and when I do you'll have something to talk about.'

'I'm sure I shall,' said Mr Reeder.

'There's a time to be 'igh and mighty, and a time to be 'umble,' Buckingham went on mysteriously. 'That's all I've got to say – there's a time to be 'igh and mighty, and a time to be 'umble!'

The Oracle of Delphi could not have been more profound.

A second later Mr Reeder saw him talking to a little man with a hard and unprepossessing face. Evidently the man was not a member of the audience, for later Mr Reeder saw him going out through the main entrance.

'Who is he?' asked Larry when the man had gone.

'I haven't the least idea,' said Reeder, and Larry chuckled.

'You've one thing in common at any rate,' he said; 'You both think classical music is muck. I'm going to give up trying to educate you.'

Mr Reeder was very apologetic after the concert. He liked music, but music of a kind. He had a weakness for the popular airs of twenty-five years ago, and confessed a little shamefacedly that he occasionally hummed these favourite tunes of his in his bath.

'Not that I can sing.'

'I'm sure of that,' said Larry.

Two days later Mr Reeder saw the two men again. It was on the north side of Westminster Bridge. Immediately opposite the Houses of Parliament there was a traffic block. At this point the road was being repaired and the police were marshalling the traffic into a single line.

Mr Reeder was waiting to cross the road and was examining the vehicles that passed. To say that he was examining them idly would not have been true. He never examined anything idly. He saw a new grey van and glanced up at the driver. It was the thin-faced man he had seen in the Queen's Hall bar, and by his side sat Buckingham.

Neither of the men saw him as they passed. Mr Reeder could guess by the movement of the body that the van carried a fairly heavy load, for the springs were strained and the strain on the engine was almost perceptible.

Odd, thought Mr Reeder ... van drivers

and their assistants do not as a rule choose concert halls as meeting places. But then, so many things in life were odd. For example: it was a very curious friendship that had developed between himself and Larry. Reeder was the soul of rectitude. He had never in his life committed one act that could be regarded by the most rigid of moralists as dishonest. He had chosen, for the one friend he had ever had, a man who had only just escaped imprisonment, was undoubtedly a burglar, as undoubtedly the possessor of a large fortune which he had stolen from the interests which it was Mr Reeder's duty to protect.

Such thoughts occurred to J.G Reeder in such odd moments of contemplation as when he shaved himself or was brushing his teeth; but he had no misgiving, was unrepentant. He looked upon all criminals as a normal-minded doctor looks upon patients; they were beings who required specialised attention when they were in the grip of their peculiar malady, and were amongst the normals of life when they were cured.

And to be cured, from Mr Reeder's point of view, was to undergo a special treatment in Wormwood Scrubbs, Dartmoor, Parkhurst, Maidstone, or whatever prison was adaptable for the treatment of those who suffered from, or caused, social disorders.

The next time Larry called, which was on a Sunday a fortnight later, he had an adventure to tell.

'Respect me as a reformed crook, and salute me as a hero,' he said extravagantly, as he hung up his coat. 'I've saved a distressed damsel from death! With that rare presence of mind which is the peculiar possession of the O'Ryans, I was able–'

'It wasn't so much presence of mind as a lamp-post,' murmured Mr Reeder; 'though I grant that you were – um – quick on the – shall I say, uptake? In this case "uptake" is the right word.'

Larry stared at him.

'Did you see it?' he asked.

'I was an interested spectator,' said Mr Reeder. 'It happened very near to my office, and I was looking out of the window at that moment. I fear I waste a great deal of time looking out of the window, but I find the traffic of Whitehall intensely interesting. A car got out of control and swerved onto the pavement. It was going beyond the ordinary speed limit, and the young lady would, I think, have been severely injured if you had not lifted her aside just before the car crashed into the lamp-post. As it was, she had a very narrow escape. I applauded you, but silently, because the rules of the office call for quiet. But I still think the lamp-post had almost as much to do with it–'

'Of course it had, but she might have been hurt. Did you see her?' asked Larry eagerly. 'She's lovely! God, how lovely!'

Mr Reeder thought she was interesting, and said so. Larry scoffed.

'Interesting! She's marvellous! She has the face and figure of an angel – and don't tell me you've never met an angel – and she has a voice like custard. I was so knocked off my feet by her that she thought I was hurt.'

Mr Reeder nodded.

'I saw her. In fact, I – er – looked rather closely at her. I keep a small pair of field glasses on my desk, and I'm afraid I was rather inquisitive. Who is she?'

Larry shook his head.

'I don't know. I didn't ask her her name, naturally: she was rather upset by what had happened, and she hurried off. I saw her get into a Rolls-Royce that was evidently waiting for her–'

'Yes,' said Mr Reeder. 'I saw the Rolls. It is a pity.'

'It *is* a pity. If I'd had any sense I'd have

43

told her my name. After all, the least she can do is to write and thank her brave preserver.'

'She may yet – no, no, I wasn't thinking of that.'

The housekeeper came in and laid the table, and during the operation Mr Reeder was silent. When she had gone: 'I wasn't thinking of that,' he went on, as though there had been no interruption of his thoughts. 'I was thinking that if you had been properly introduced you might have asked her why such a strong safe was ordered.'

Larry looked at him blankly.

'Strong safe? I don't know what you're talking about.'

Mr Reeder smiled. It pleased him to mystify this clever young man.

'The lady's name was Miss Lane Leonard,' he said.

Larry frowned.

'Do you know her?'

'I have never seen her before in my life.'

'Then how the devil do you know she was Miss Lane Leonard? Have you seen her picture–?'

Mr Reeder shook his head.

'I've never seen a picture of her. I have

neither seen her since nor before; I have received no information from any person immediately concerning her identity.'

'Then how the devil do you know?' asked the astonished Larry.

Mr Reeder chuckled.

'A person who has a car number has also a name. I was interested to discover who she was, 'phoned across to Scotland Yard, and they supplied me with the name that is attached to that particular car number. Miss Lane Leonard, 409 Berkeley Square, and Sevenways Castle, Sevenways, Kent. 409 Berkeley Square, by the way, is an expensive block of residential flats, so that if you feel that she would be happier for knowing the name of her – um – brave deliverer – I think that was the phrase – you might drop her a line and explain, with whatever modesty you can command, just how much she owes to you.'

Larry was very thoughtful.

'That's queer. Do you remember we were talking about the Lane Leonards' strong-room only a few weeks ago, and wondering why such an expensive contraption had been ordered. A lady worth a couple of millions.'

'I'm sorry,' Mr Reeder smiled. 'I've spoilt your romance. You would have preferred that she were poor – um – but honest. That her father, or preferably her mother, was in the grip of a cruel – um – usurer, and that you might have rescued her once more with the magnificent capital which you have acquired by illicit and altogether disreputable means.'

Larry went red. He was a dreamer, and he was annoyed that anybody should know him as such, so annoyed that he abruptly changed the subject.

It was that night for the first time that J.G Reeder learned the story of Larry O'Ryan's boyhood, and the circumstances which had determined him in his career.

'I'm glad you've told me, Mr O'Ryan.' Curiously enough, during all the years he knew Larry he never addressed him in any other way.) 'It makes you more understandable than I thought you were, and excuses, as far as abnormal tendencies can be excused, your subsequent – um – behaviour. You should, of course, have gone to the head master and told the truth, and probably in later years, since thinking the matter over, you have come to the same conclusions.'

Larry nodded.

'Have you met the man since – the master who stole the money?'

'No,' said Larry, 'but I should have probably met him if I had made Wormwood Scrubbs en route to Dartmoor. Only a born crook could have stolen from Farthingale, who was a good-hearted soul and hadn't too much money. I sent him a monkey by the way, last week. His wife's had an operation, and I know the little man hasn't a great deal of money.'

'A monkey being twenty-five or five hundred pounds? I have never quite accustomed myself to these sporting terms,' asked Mr Reeder. 'Five hundred pounds? Well, well, it is nice to be generous with other people's money, but we won't go into that.'

He sat, drumming his fingers on the table.

'Once a crook, always a crook – that is your real belief, Mr O'Ryan? But at heart you're not a crook. You're just a young man who thought that he was taking the law into his own hands and was perfectly justified in doing so, which of course is absurd. If everybody thought as you do – but I am getting on to a very old and a tedious subject.'

The telephone bell rang shrilly. Mr Reeder walked to his desk, picked up the receiver and listened, answering monosyllabically.

When he had finished: 'I'm afraid our evening is going to be spoilt, Mr O'Ryan. I am wanted at the office.'

'It must be something very important to take you up on Sunday evening,' said O'Ryan.

'Everything that comes to me from the office is very important, on Sunday evening or even Monday evening,' said Reeder.

He took up the telephone directory, called a number and gave explicit and urgent instructions.

'If you're hiring a car, it *is* important!'

Mr Reeder inclined his head.

'It is rather a matter of urgency,' he said. 'It is, in fact – um – a murder.'

4

On this Sunday morning a policeman patrolling the very edge of the Metropolitan area, at that point near Slough where the County of Buckinghamshire and the County of London meet, had seen a foot sticking up apparently from the grass. It was in a place where no foot should have been, a rough, uneven field, crossed by an irrigation ditch which was now dry. The fact that there was a ditch there was unknown to the policeman until he opened a gate leading into the field and investigated.

As he opened the gate he noticed the marks of car wheels leading into the field, and saw that the padlocked chain which fastened the gate to a post had been broken. The policeman noticed this mechanically. He crossed the rough ground, wet with recent rain and came to the ditch, and the mystery of the foot was revealed. A man lay there on his back. He was dressed in his underclothes and a pair of socks, and one glance at the face told the policeman what had happened.

He hailed a passing motorist and sent him off to the station to procure assistance. A police surgeon and an ambulance arrived, and the body was removed. Within an hour Scotland Yard was working on the case.

They had little guidance for their investigations. The man's clothes were innocent even of laundry marks; there was nothing whatever to assist in his identification. The curious fact which struck the investigating officers was that the underclothes were silk, though the man himself was evidently a workman, for his hands were rough and his general physique and appearance suggested that he belonged to the labouring rather than to the leisured classes.

Experts who examined the car tracks could throw no light upon the subject. It had been a big car, and presumably the hour at which the body had been deposited was between two and four o'clock in the morning. By the curve of the track the police decided that the car had come from the direction of London. That was all that was known about it. Cars on the Bath Road are frequent on a Saturday night, and no patrolling policeman had seen the vehicle turning into the field.

One thing was clear to Mr Reeder the moment he had the facts in his possession, which was not until very late that afternoon, and it was that the car owner must have reconnoitred the spot and decided exactly where the body was to be deposited. He must have known of the existence of the chain which held the gate, and of the ditch beyond.

The field was the property of a small company which was buying land in the neighbourhood – the Land Development Corporation, which had an office in the City. Its business was to buy suitable building sites and to resell them on easy payments.

It was growing dark by the time Mr Reeder finished his personal investigations.

'And now,' he said, 'I think I would like to see this unfortunate man.'

They took him to the shed where the murdered man lay, and the Inspector in charge gave him the gist of the doctor's report.

'He was beaten over the head, his skull fractured; there is no other sign of injury, but the doctor said these are quite sufficient to cause almost instantaneous death. An iron bar must have been used, or something equally heavy.'

Mr Reeder said nothing. He went out of the shed, and waited while the door was padlocked.

'If we can only get him identified–' began the Inspector.

'I can identify him,' said Mr Reeder quietly. 'His name is Buckingham – he is an ex-constable of the Metropolitan Police Force.'

Within two hours Reeder was examining Buckingham's record in the Inspector's office at Scotland Yard. It was not a particularly good one. The man had served for twelve years in the Metropolitan Police Force and had been six times reprimanded for conduct prejudicial to discipline and on one occasion had narrowly escaped expulsion from the force. He had a history of drunkenness, had twice been before the Commissioner accused of receiving bribes, once from a bookmaker and once from a man whom he had arrested and had subsequently released. Eventually he had retired, without pension, to take up a position in the country. Particulars of that position were not available, and the only information on file was his last address.

Reeder charged himself with this investigation, he went to a small house in Southwark, discovered Buckingham's wife living there and broke to her the news of her husband's death. She accepted the fact very calmly, indeed philosophically. ❧

'I haven't seen him for three or four years,' she said. 'The only money he ever sent me was ten pounds last Christmas, and I wouldn't have got that only I met him in the street with a girl – and a sick-looking creature she was! – and had a row with him.'

She was a little inconsistent in her indignation, for she told him quite calmly that she had married again, relying upon a law which is known only to the poor and certainly unknown to any lawyer, that if a husband deserts a wife and is not seen for two years she may marry again. And Mrs Buckingham had undoubtedly married again.

Mr Reeder was not concerned with this blatant act of bigamy, but pressed her as to where the man had been employed. Here he came against a blank wall. Her husband had told her nothing, and apparently throughout their married life his attitude had been one of reticence, particularly with regard to his financial position and his private affairs.

'He was a bad husband to me. He's dead, and I don't want to say anything against him. But I'm telling you, Mr Whatever-your-name-is, that I'm not going into mourning for him. He's deserted me three times in my married life, and once he gave me a black eye, and I've never forgiven him for that. It was my right eye,' she added.

Mr Reeder could wonder if there were any greater enormity in blacking the right than the left eye, but he did not pursue inquiries in this direction.

All the woman could tell him was that her husband had taken a job in the country, that he was making a lot of money, and that when she had seen him in town he was 'dressed flash, like a gentleman.'

'When I say a gentleman,' she said, 'he might have been a waiter. He had a white shirt-front on and a black tie, and he was looking as though he'd come into a fortune. Otherwise I wouldn't have asked him for any money.'

So far as she knew, he had no friends; at any rate, she could not supply the name of any person from whom particulars of his life might be secured.

'When you say he worked in the country, which part of the country? Have you any idea what station he came from or went to?' he persisted.

She thought a while.

'Yes, Charing Cross. My brother saw him

54

there one night, about two years ago.'

She had none of his belongings, no notebook or papers of any kind.

'Not even,' she said, 'as much as a tobacco tin.'

She had cut herself completely and absolutely adrift from him, never wanted to hear from or see him again, and her accidental meeting with him in the street was only to be remembered because it was so profitable.

Mr Reeder returned to headquarters, to consult with investigators who had followed other lines of inquiry, and learned that they too had come to a dead end. J.G Reeder was puzzled and exhilarated, and could have wished that he controlled the inquiries instead of being an independent seeker after knowledge.

Here was a man, an ex-policeman, so prosperous that he could afford the finest silken underwear, found in a field, with no marks to identify him, obviously murdered, obviously conveyed from the scene of the murder by a car and deposited in the dark in a ditch which only those closely acquainted with the ground could have known existed.

There was another woman in London who could give him information: the 'highbrow lady' with the pallid face, who loved classical music and strong drink. London would be combed for her; there was a possibility that she might easily be found.

The next morning he went early to the concert hall and interviewed the attendant. Mr Reeder might know little about music, but he knew something about music-lovers, and if this woman was a regular concert-goer, the attendant might remember her. Fortune was with him, for two men knew her, one by name. She was a Miss Letzfeld and she was especially to be remembered because she suffered from an inferiority complex, believed that attendants deliberately slighted her and pestered the management with letters of complaint. By luck, one of these letters had been kept. Miss Letzfeld lived at Breddleston Mews in Kensington.

Mr Reeder went straight to the address and, after repeated knockings, gained the attention of the occupant. She came down to open the door, rather unpleasant to see in the clean daylight. A thin, long-faced girl, with sleepy eyes and an ugly mouth, wrapped in a dingy dressing gown.

To his surprise she recognised him.

'Your name's Reeder, isn't it? Didn't Billy

introduce you – at the Queen's Hall? You're a detective, aren't you?' And then, quickly: 'Is anything wrong?' ⊙

'May I come up?' he asked.

She led the way up the narrow stairs, her high-heeled shoes drumming unmusically on the bare, uncarpeted treads.

The room into which he was ushered was expensively furnished, but most cheaply maintained. The untidy remnants of a meal were on a table. The room gave him the impression that it had neither been dusted nor swept for a week. Over one chair were a few articles of women's apparel, which she snatched up.

'I want to say this, Mr Reeder,' she said, almost before he was in the room, 'that if there is anything wrong I know nothing about it. Billy's been very good to me, but he's trying. I don't know how he got his money, and I've never asked him.'

To Mr Reeder fell the unpleasant duty of telling her of the fate that had overtaken her man, and again he found that the tragic end of ex-Constable Buckingham evoked no very violent emotions. She was shocked, but impersonally shocked.

'That's terrible, isn't it?' she said breathlessly. 'Billy was such a good boy' (the

57

description sounded a little ludicrous even in that tragic moment), 'though he wasn't what you might call particularly intellectual. I only saw him now and again, once a fortnight, sometimes once a week.'

'Where did he come from?' asked Reeder.

She shook her head.

'I don't know. He never told me things; he was very close about his private life. He worked in the country for a very rich man. I don't even know what part of the county it was.'

'Had he plenty of money?'

'You mean Billy? Yes, he always had plenty of money, and lived well. He had an office in the city somewhere, something to do with land. I wouldn't have known that, but I saw a telegram that he left behind here one day. It was addressed to the Something Land Corporation, but it wasn't in his own name–'

'The Land Development Corporation?' asked Mr Reeder quickly. 'Do you remember the address?'

The girl wasn't sure, but she knew it was in the City.

She had nothing of the man's in her possession except – and here was the most important discovery – a photograph of

Buckingham taken a year before. With this in his possession Mr Reeder drove to the City.

The Land Development Corporation had an office in one of the big blocks near the Mansion House. It consisted of one room, in which a clerk and a typist worked, and a smaller room, very plainly furnished, where the Managing Director sat on his infrequent visits.

For an hour Mr Reeder plied clerk and typist with questions, and when he got back to Scotland Yard he was in possession of so many facts that contradicted one another, so many that were entirely irreconcilable, that he found it difficult to put them in sequence.

The plain, matter-of-fact report which he put before his superior may be quoted in full.

'In the case of William Buckingham. Line of investigation, Land Development Corporation. This corporation was registered as a private company two years ago. It has a capital of £1,000 and debentures amounting to £300,000. The Directors are the clerk and the typist and a Mr William Buck. The bank balance is £1,300, and the company is proprietor of a large number of land blocks situated in the south of England, and evidently purchased with the object of development. A considerable number of these have been resold. Mr Buck was undoubtedly Buckingham. He came to the office very rarely, only to sign cheques. Large sums of money have been paid into and withdrawn from the bank, and a superficial inspection of the books suggests that these were genuine transactions. A further examination, necessarily of a hurried character, reveals considerable gaps in the accounting. The field where the body of Buckingham was found is part of the property of this company, and obviously Buckingham would be well acquainted with the land, though it is a curious fact that he had been there recently twice by night...'

5

The next morning a portrait of Buckingham appeared in every London newspaper, together with such particulars as would assist in a further identification. No news came until the afternoon of that day. Mr Reeder was in his office, examining documents in relation to a large and illicit importation of cocaine, when a messenger came in with a card. 'Major Digby Olbude,' it read, and in the left-hand corner: 'Lane Leonard Estate Office, Sevenways Castle, Sevenways, Kent'.

Mr Reeder sat back in his chair, adjusted his unnecessary glasses and read the card again.

'Ask Major Olbude to come up,' he said.

Major Obude was tall, florid, white of hair, rather pedantic of speech.

'I have come to see you about the man Buckingham. I understand you are in charge of the investigations?'

Mr Reeder bowed. It was not the moment to direct what might prove an interesting and informative caller to the man who was legitimately entitled to have first-hand information.

'Will you sit down, Major?'

He rose, pushed a chair forward for the visitor, and Major Olbude pulled up the knees of his creased trousers carefully and sat down.

'I saw the portrait in this morning's newspaper – at least, my niece drew my attention to it – and I came up at once, because I feel it is my duty, and the duty, indeed, of every good citizen to assist the police even in the smallest particular in a case of this importance.'

'Very admirable,' murmured Mr Reeder.

'Buckingham was in my service; he was one of the guards of what the local people call the treasure house of Sevenways Castle.'

Again Mr Reeder nodded, as though he knew all that was to be known about Sevenways Castle.

'As I say, my niece reads the newspapers, a practice in which I do not indulge, for in these days of sensationalism there is very little in newspapers in which an intellectual man finds the least pleasure and instruction. Buckingham had been in the employment of the late Mr Lane Leonard, and on Mr

Lane Leonard's death his services were transferred to myself, Mr Lane Leonard's brother-in-law and his sole trustee. I might say that Mr Lane Leonard, as everybody knows, died very suddenly of heart failure and left behind a considerable fortune, eighty per cent of which was in bullion.'

'In gold?' asked Mr Reeder, surprised.

The major inclined his head.

'That was my brother-in-law's eccentricity. He had amassed this enormous sum of money by speculation, and lived in terror that it should be dissipated by his descendants – unhappily, he has only a daughter to carry on his name – in the same manner as it was amassed. He also took a very pessimistic view of the future of civilisation and particularly of the English race. He believed – and here I think he was justified – that for ten years there would be no industrial development in the country, and that English securities would fall steadily. He had a very rooted objection to banks, and the upshot of it all was that he accumulated in his lifetime a sum in gold equivalent to over a million and a half pounds. This was kept, and is still kept, in a chamber which he had specially built practically within the walls of the castle, and to guard which he engaged a staff of ex-policemen, one of whom is on duty every hour of the day and night. It is unnecessary for me to tell you, Mr Reeder, a man with a commercial knowledge, that by this method my brother-in-law was depriving his daughter of a very considerable income, the interest at five per cent on a million and a half being seventy-five thousand pounds per annum. In ten years that would be three-quarters of a million, so that the provisions of this will mean that nearly four hundred thousand pounds is lost to my ward, and almost as much to the Treasury.'

'Very distressing,' said Mr Reeder, and shook his head mournfully, as though the thought of the Treasury losing money cut him to the quick.

'There is a separate fund invested in high-class government security,' the major went on, 'on which my niece and myself live. Naturally, the custody of such an enormous sum is a source of constant anxiety to me – in fact, only two years ago I ordered an entirely new strongroom to be built at a very considerable cost.'

He paused.

'And Buckingham?' asked Mr Reeder gently. 'I will come to Buckingham,' said the major with great dignity. 'He was one of the guards employed. There are in all seven. Each lives in his own quarters, and it is against the rules I have instituted that these men should meet except when they relieve one another of their post. The practice is for the guard on duty to ring a bell communicating with the quarters of his relief, who immediately comes to the treasure house and, after being identified, is admitted. Buckingham should have come on duty at six o'clock on Saturday night. His predecessor at the post rang the bell as usual, but Buckingham did not appear. After an hour the man communicated with me, by telephone – there is a telephone connection between my study and the dome – I call it the dome because of its shape – and I set immediately to find the missing man. His room was empty, there was no sign of him, and I ordered the emergency man to take his place.'

'Since then you have not seen him?'

The major shook his head.

'No, sir. Nor have I heard from him.'

'What salary did you pay this man?'

'Ten pounds a week, quarters, lighting and food. All the guards were supplied from the kitchen of the castle.'

'Had he any private means?'

'None,' said the other emphatically.

'Would you be surprised to know that he has been speculating heavily in land?' asked Mr Reeder.

The major rose to his feet, not quickly, but with a certain stately deliberation.

'I should be both surprised and horrified,' he said. 'Is there any way by which he could have had access to the – um – treasure house?'

'No, sir,' said Olbude, 'no method whatever, except through the door, of which I hold the key. The wall is made of concrete twelve inches thick and lined with half-inch steel. The locks are unpickable.'

'And the foundations?' suggested Mr Reeder.

'Eight feet of solid concrete. It is absolutely impossible.'

Mr Reeder rubbed his chin, looking down at the desk, his lips drooping dismally.

'Do you often go into the – um – treasure house?'

'Yes, sir, I go in every month, on the first day of every month. In other words, I was there last Friday.'

'And nothing had been disturbed?'

'Nothing,' said the other emphatically.

'I presume the bullion is in steel boxes–'

'In large glass containers. That was another of Mr Lane Leonard's eccentricities. There are about six hundred of these, each containing two thousand five hundred pounds' worth of gold. It is possible to see at a glance whether the money has been disturbed. The containers are hermetically closed and sealed. They stand on reinforced concrete shelves, in eight tiers, on three sides of the treasure house, each tier holding seventy-five containers. The treasure house, I may explain, consists of two buildings; the inner shell, which is the treasure house proper, and another separate building, as it were a box placed over this to give protection to the guard and sufficient space for them to promenade. The outer building contains a small kitchenette, with tables, chairs and the necessary accommodation for the comfort of the guard. Attached to this is a lobby, also guarded with a steel door, and beyond that an iron grille, above which is a powerful electric light to enable the inner guard to scrutinise his relief and make sure that he is the right man – that is to say, that he is not being impersonated.'

Mr Reeder was a little puzzled, but only a little.

'Very extraordinary,' he said, 'can you tell me any more about Buckingham?'

The major hesitated.

'No, except that he went to town more frequently than any of the other guards. For this I was responsible, I am afraid! I gave him greater freedom because he was the doyen of the guards in point of service.'

'Extraordinary,' said Mr Reeder again.

The story had its fantastical and improbable side, and yet J.G Reeder regarded it as being no more than – extraordinary. Misers there had been since there were valuable things to hoard. Every nation had its safe place where unproductive gold was hoarded. He knew of at least three similar cases of men who had maintained in vaults vast sums in bullion.

'I should like to come down to – um – Sevenways Castle and see this man's quarters,' he said. 'It will be necessary to go through his possessions. Had he any friends?'

The major nodded.

'He had a friend, I believe, in London – a girl. I don't know who she was. To tell you the truth, Mr Reeder, I have an idea that he was married, though he never spoke of his wife. But what were you telling me about his having money? That is news to me.'

J.G Reeder scratched his chin and hesitated.

'I am not quite sure whether I have absolute authority for saying that he was the head of a certain land corporation, but as his staff have recognised his photograph–'

He sketched the story of the Land Development Company, and Major Olbude listened without interruption.

'Then it was in one of his own fields that he was found? When I say his own fields, I mean on land which he himself owned. That is amazing. I am afraid I can tell you no more about him,' he said, as he took up his hat and stick, 'but of course I am available whenever you wish to question me. There may be some things about him that I have forgotten, but I will write my telephone number on your card and you may call me up.'

He did this with his pencil, Mr Reeder standing by and watching the process with interest.

He accompanied his guest down the stairs into Whitehall, and arrived in time to witness a peculiar incident. A Rolls was drawn up by the kerb and three persons were standing by it. He recognised the girl instantly. Larry's back was towards him, but he had no difficulty in identifying the broad shoulders of that young man. The third member of the party was evidently the chauffeur. He was red of face, talking and gesticulating violently. Mr Reeder heard him say: 'You've got no right to speak to the young lady, and if you want to talk, talk in English so as I can understand you.'

The major quickened his pace, crossed to the group and spoke sharply to the chauffeur.

'Why are you making a scene?' he demanded.

Larry O'Ryan had walked away, a surprising circumstance, for Larry was the sort that never walked away from trouble of any kind.

Mr Reeder came up to the group. The major could do no less than introduce him.

'This is my niece, Miss Lane Leonard,' he said.

She was lovely; even Mr Reeder, who was no connoisseur, acknowledged the fresh beauty of the girl. He thought she was rather pale, and wondered whether that was her natural colour.

'What is the trouble, my dear?' asked the major.

70

'I met a friend – the man who saved me from being run over by a motor car,' she said jerkily. 'I spoke to him in – in French.'

'He speaks English all right,' growled the unpleasant-looking chauffeur.

'Will you be quiet! Was that all, my dear?'

She nodded.

'You thanked him, I suppose? I remember you telling me that you did not have the opportunity of thanking him before. He went away before you could speak to him. Modesty in a young man is most admirable. And it was in Whitehall that it happened?'

'Yes,' she nodded.

Mr Reeder felt that she was looking at him, although her eyes were fixed upon her uncle. He saw something else; her gloved hand was trembling. She was trying hard to control it, but it trembled.

The major turned and shook hands with him.

'I shall probably be seeing you again, Mr Reeder,' he said.

He turned abruptly, helped the girl into the car and the machine drew away. Reeder looked round for Larry, saw him staring intently into a doorway, and as the car passed him, saw him turn so that his back was to the vehicle.

Larry walked quickly towards him.

'Sorry,' he said; 'but I wanted to see you and I was hanging around till you came out.'

His eyes were bright; his whole attitude was tense, electric; he seemed charged with some suppressed excitement.

'You met the young lady?'

'Yes. Interesting, isn't she?'

'Why didn't you stay and meet her uncle?'

'Rather embarrassing – fine-looking old boy. Perhaps I was a little conscience-stricken. That chauffeur...'

He was not smiling; his eyes were hard, his lips were set straight.

'He never had a narrower escape than he did today. Have you ever wanted to kill somebody, Mr Reeder? I've never had it before – just a brutal desire to maim and beat, and mutilate–'

'Why did you speak in French?'

'It's my favourite language,' said Larry glibly. 'Anyway, she might have been French; she's got the chic of a Parisienne and the loveliness of an Italian dawn.'

Mr Reeder looked at him oddly.

'Why are you being so mysterious?' he asked.

'Am I?' Larry laughed. There was a note of

hysteria in that laugh. The bright look had come back to his eyes. 'I wonder if he did?'

'Did what?' asked Mr Reeder, but the young man answered him with a question.

'Are you going down to call on our friend? By the way, did he employ the man Buckingham?'

'What do you know about Buckingham?' asked Mr Reeder slowly.

'It's in the papers this morning. I mean the man who was killed.'

'Did you know him?'

Larry shook his head.

'No. I've seen his portrait – a common-place-looking hombre, hardly worth murdering, do you think? Lord, Mr Reeder, isn't it great to be alive!'

A few spots of rain were falling. Mr Reeder was conscious of the fact that he was bareheaded.

'Come up to my office,' he said. 'I'll take the risk of being – um – reprimanded by my superior.'

Larry hesitated.

'All right, I'm all for it,' he said, and followed Mr Reeder up the stairs.

J.G shut the door and pointed to a chair. 'Why the excitement?' he asked. 'Why the – um – champing of bits, as it were?'

73

Larry sat back in his chair and folded his arms tightly.

'I've got an idea I'm being six kinds of a fool for not taking you entirely into my confidence, but here's adventure, Mr Reeder, the most glorious adventure that can come to a young man of courage and enterprise. And I think I'll spoil it a little if I tell you. I'll ask you one favour: was the major wearing his glasses when he came into the street?'

Mr Reeder nodded.

'I don't remember that he took them off,' he said.

Larry frowned and bit his lip.

'I'll tell you something. Do you remember when I lifted that young lady out of the way of a car? It was right outside this office, wasn't it? She had just left her own car, and left it rather hurriedly, and was coming – where do you think? To this office, no less! She didn't tell me so, but I'm pretty sure that was where she was bound. And the chauffeur was flying after her. I didn't realise it at the time, but I realise it now. On the day before that happened there was an article in the *Megaphone* about you, rather a eulogistic one, and a pencil sketch of you. Do you remember?'

Mr Reeder blushed.

'There was rather a stupid – um – ill-informed – um–'

'Exactly. It was rather flattering. I don't know how flattering it was, but your own conscience will tell you. I worked it out in two seconds; that was why she was coming to see you. This misguided and ill-informed writer in the *Megaphone* said you were the greatest detective of the age, or something of the sort. It probably isn't true, though I'll hand you all sorts of bouquets on a gold plate, for you certainly embarrassed me on one never-to-be forgotten occasion. And she read it, found out where your office was – anyway, she wants to see you now. She said that much.'

'Wants to see me?' said Mr Reeder incredulously. Larry nodded. 'Isn't it amazing! I couldn't have been speaking to her for more than a minute, and she's the beginning and end of life to me.'

He got up and began to pace the room excitedly.

'To me, Mr Reeder, a crook of crooks, a burglar. But she's worth a million and a half, and absolutely unreachable. I couldn't propose to her. But if she said, "Walk into the middle of Westminster Bridge and jump into the river," I'd do it!'

Mr Reeder stared at him.

'It almost sounds as though you like her very much,' he said.

'It almost does,' said Larry savagely.

He stopped in his stride, pointed a finger of his extended hand towards Mr Reeder.

'I'm not going to jump from the middle of Westminster Bridge. It's a far, far better thing that I do – or rather, I'm going to do a far, far better thing, and it's going to make all the difference in life to me if I succeed.'

'If you will sit down,' said Mr Reeder mildly, 'and talk a little less obscurely, perhaps I could assist you.'

Larry shook his head.

'No; I've got to blaze my own trail.' He chuckled. 'My metaphors are a bit mixed, but then, so is my mind. When are you going to Sevenways Castle?'

'She told you she lived there, did she?' asked Mr Reeder.

'When are you going?'

J.G considered.

'Tomorrow – tomorrow afternoon probably.' And then: 'You don't know Buckingham?'

'No,' said Larry. 'I recognised him, of course, as the fellow who came up and spoke to you when we were at the Queen's Hall. Odd coincidence, meeting him at all, wasn't it?'

He walked to the door and opened it.

'I'll go now, Mr Reeder, if you'll excuse me. Perhaps I'll call and see you tonight. By the way, are you in the American market?'

'I never speculate,' said Reeder primly. 'I don't think I have bought a stock or a share in my life, and certainly I should not buy now, I read the papers, of course, and I see the market is down.'

'And how!' said Larry cryptically.

He was a little confusing. His reference to the stock market interested Mr Reeder to the extent of inducing him to wade through the tape prices that night. Stock was falling rapidly in Wall Street; there was panic selling and gloomy forecasts of a complete collapse. He could only wonder how Larry's mercurial mind could have leapt to this mundane fact in his emotional moment.

He had a considerable amount of work to do that afternoon, inquiries to pursue at certain banks, reports to read and digest, and it was nearly nine o'clock before he went home, so tired that he fell asleep almost before he pulled the covers over his shoulders.

6

Pamela Lane Leonard drove back into Kent that morning, silent, resentful, a little frightened.

'Why do you allow Lidgett to talk to you like that, Uncle Digby?' she asked.

Major Digby Olbude blinked and looked at her. 'Like what, my dear?' he asked irritably. 'Lidgett is an old friend of the family, and retainers have certain privileges.'

'Did you tell Mr Reeder that he and Buckingham had quarrelled?'

Olbude did not answer for a while.

'I wasn't aware that they had quarrelled,' he said, 'and I certainly should not have told Mr Reeder – how do you come to be acquainted with Mr Reeder?'

She shook her head.

'I'm not acquainted with him. I've read a lot about him – he's very clever.' And then: 'Why do you allow Lidgett to talk to you so rudely, and why do you let him talk to me as if I were – well, a servant?'

The major drew a long breath.

'You're altogether mistaken, my dear. Lidgett is a little uncouth, but he's a very faithful servant. I will speak to him.'

Another long silence.

'When did they quarrel – Buckingham and Lidgett, I mean?' asked Olbude.

'I saw them in the woods one day. Buckingham knocked him down.'

Olbude ran his fingers through his grey hair.

'It is all very difficult,' he said. 'Your lamented father gave special instructions to me that on no account was Lidgett to be discharged; and until you are twenty-five I am afraid you have no voice in the matter, my dear.'

Then, suddenly:

'What did you say to that young man?'

This was the second time he had asked the question. 'I've told you,' she answered shortly. 'He's the man who saved me from being killed by a car, and I thanked him.'

She was not telling the truth, but her conscience was curiously clear.

There was something she wanted to tell him, but she could not. The very fact that the man she hated and feared was sitting within a yard of her, beyond the glass panel which separated chauffeur from passenger, was sufficient to stop her; it was Olbude who returned to the subject.

'Lidgett is a rough diamond. You've got to put his loyalty in the scale against his uncouthness, Pamela. He is devoted to the family–'

'He is devoted to me!' she said, her voice trembling with indignation. 'Are you aware, Uncle Digby, that this man has asked me to marry him?'

He turned to her, open-mouthed.

'Asked you to marry him?' he said incredulously. 'He actually asked you? I told him that in no circumstances was he to dare mention such a thing–'

It was her turn to be amazed.

'Surely he hasn't discussed it with you? And did you listen to him? Oh, no! Didn't you – uncle, what did you do?'

He moved uneasily, avoiding her eyes.

'He's a rough diamond,' he repeated in a low voice. 'There is a lot about Lidgett which is very admirable. Naturally, he is not particularly well educated, and he's twenty years older than you, but he's a man with many great qualities.'

She could only subside helplessly in the corner of her seat and regard him with wondering eyes. He might have thought that she was impressed by his eulogy, for he went on.

'Lidgett is a man who has saved a lot of money. In fact, I think, thanks to the generosity of your stepfather, Lidgett is very rich. And the disparity of your ages isn't really as important as it appears.'

Then, as a thought struck him, he asked quickly: 'You didn't tell O'Ryan this?'

'O'Ryan?' she repeated. 'Do you know him?'

'You seem to,' he answered quickly. 'Did he tell you his name in the few seconds you saw him?'

She nodded.

'Yes, he told me his name. Where did you meet him?'

He evaded the question.

'That's neither here nor there. I don't suppose he knows me. He was quite a child when I saw him last – he didn't say he knew me, did he?' he asked anxiously.

She shook her head.

'No, we hardly discussed you.'

'What did you discuss?' he asked.

She hesitated.

'Nothing that would interest you,' she said.

She went straight to her room when she

arrived, and sat down to write a letter. It would probably go the way of other letters she had written; the servants of Sevenways were completely dominated by Lidgett, and she knew by experience that every letter she wrote passed through his hands.

The situation was an intolerable one, but she had grown up in it. Ever since she had returned from school, Lidgett had been master of the house, and her uncle the merest cipher. It was Lidgett who chose the servants, Lidgett who discharged them without reference to his employer; Lidgett took out the car when he wanted it, even ordered improvements to the estate without consulting his employer.

He had walked into the drawing room one afternoon when she was reading, and without preliminary had put his monstrous proposal.

'I dare say this is going to shock you, Miss Pamela, but I've saved a bit of money and want to get married, and I'm in love with you, and that's the beginning and end of it.'

'With me?' She could hardly believe her ears.

'That's the idea,' he said coolly. 'I haven't talked the matter over with the major, but don't think he'll object. Lots of ladies have married their chauffeurs, and I will make you as good a husband as any of these la-di-dah fellows you are likely to meet.'

That had been the proposal, in almost exactly those words. She had been too staggered to make an adequate reply.

She was desperate now. Lidgett made no disguise of his dominant position. He had dared even in the presence of Larry to order her into her car and, even as she was writing, there came a knock at her door and his hateful voice called her. She put the letter hastily between sheets of blotting paper, unlocked the door and opened it.

'What was that fellow saying to you in French?' he asked.

'What he said was unimportant, Lidgett,' she said quietly. 'It is what I said that mattered. I told him that I was virtually a prisoner in this house, that you were in control and had asked me to marry you. I told him I was terribly afraid, and asked him to communicate with the police.'

His face went red, livid, then a sickly white.

'Oh, you did, did you?' His voice was high and squeaky. 'That's what you said – told lies about me!'

He was frightened; she recognised the

symptoms and her heart leapt.

'The day I nearly had the accident,' she went on, 'I was on my way to see Mr Reeder, the detective. I will not be treated as you are treating me. There's something wrong in this house and I'm going to find out what it is. Major Olbude has no authority; you govern him as you govern me, and there must be some reason. Mr O'Ryan will find out what that reason is.'

'Mr O'Ryan will, will he? You know what he is, I suppose? A lag – he stood his trial for burglary. That's the kind of friend you want!'

He spoke breathlessly. Between rage and fear he was as near to being speechless as he had ever been.

'Well, we'll see about that!'

He turned on his heel and walked quickly away. She closed and locked the door. For the first time there came to her a feeling of hope. And who knew what the night would bring? For she had said something else to Larry O'Ryan, something she had not revealed to her gaoler.

Mr Reeder slept soundly, invariably for the same length of time every night. He had gone to bed a little after ten: it was a little after four when he awoke, rose, put on the kettle for his tea, and turned on the water for his bath.

At half-past four he was working at his desk. At this hour his mind was crystal-clear, and he had fewer illusions.

He had an excellent library, dealing with the peculiarities of mankind. There was one volume which he took down and skimmed rapidly. Yes, there were any number of precedents for the gold store. There was the case of Schneider, and Mr Van der Hyn, and the Polish baron Poduski, and the banker Lamonte, and that eccentric American millionaire Mr John G Grundewald – they had all been great hoarders of gold. Two of them had left wills similar to Mr Lane Leonard's. One had made so many eccentric requests in his will that the court put it aside. There was nothing remarkable, then, about Lane Leonard's distrust of stock. Mr Reeder had to confess that the latest news from America justified the caution of the dead millionaire.

He tried to reconstruct the business of Buckingham. Here was a man who acted as a guard for treasure of immense value. It could not be truly said that he had opportunities for stealing, and yet in some way he had obtained immense sums of money, and that money had been paid into the bank in gold. That was the discovery that Reeder had made on the previous afternoon. Large sums of gold had been paid into the account of the Land Development Company, as much as fifty and sixty thousand pounds at a time; so much so that the company had been asked politely to account for its possession of so much bullion, and had retorted, less politely, that if the bank did not wish to act for the directors, other banking accommodation would be found.

When could it have been stolen? The man was found dead on the Sunday, and Major Olbude had visited the vault on the Friday. Probably that morning, when he again made an inspection, Mr Reeder would receive an urgent telephone message calling him into Kent.

It began to get light. Mr Reeder pulled up the blinds and looked out into the rain-sodden street. Overhead the skies were grey and leaden. J.G brewed himself another cup of tea, and when it was made walked again to the window and stared down into the deserted thoroughfare.

He heard the whine of the car as it came round from the Lewisham High Road, pursuing a groggy course which suggested that the driver had overstayed his supper. It was a red sports car, nearly new, with a long bonnet; to Mr Reeder's surprise it finished its erratic course in front of his door. A little time passed before a man staggered out, clutching for support to the side of the car. He walked unsteadily through the gate and stumbled up the stone steps. Before he reached the door Mr Reeder was down the stairs and had opened it. He caught Larry O'Ryan in his arms and steadied him.

'I'm all right,' muttered Larry. 'I want some water. Can I sit down for a minute?'

Mr Reeder closed the door with his disengaged hand, and led the young man to the hall seat.

'I'll be all right in a second. I've lost a little blood,' muttered Larry.

The shoulders of his light mackintosh were red with it, and his face was hardly distinguishable under the broad, red streaks.

'It's all right,' he said again. 'Just a little knight-errantry.' He chuckled feebly. 'There's no fracture, though driving was rather a bother. I'm glad I didn't carry a gun – I should have used it. I think I can move now.'

He got up, swaying. Mr Reeder guided

him up the stairs through his room into the bathroom, and, soaking a towel in water, cleaned his face and the long and ugly wound beneath his matted hair.

'I think it was the chauffeur; I'm not sure. I parked the car about half a mile from Sevenways Castle, and went on foot to reconnoitre.'

All this jerkily, his head bent over a basin of red water whilst Mr Reeder applied iodine and cut away long strands of hair with a pair of office scissors.

'Anyway, I saw her.'

'You saw her?' asked Mr Reeder in astonishment. 'Yes; only for a few seconds. She couldn't get out of the window – it was barred. And the door was locked. But we had a little talk. I took a light, collapsible ladder with me to reach the window. You'll find it in a plantation near the drive.'

Mr Reeder looked at him glumly.

'Are you suggesting she is a prisoner?'

'I'm not suggesting, I'm stating the fact. An absolute prisoner. There are servants in the house, but they've all been chosen by the same man. And the best part of his money is gone.'

J.G Reeder said nothing for a while.

'How do you know?' he asked.

'I went in and looked,' was the calm reply. 'The major will probably say that I pinched it, but that was a physical impossibility. I always intended to see that treasure house – I have photographs of every key to every strongroom that the Monarch Company turned out in the last twenty years. There is a duplicate room in the office. I won't tell you how I got the photographs, because you would be pained, but I did. And I got into the treasure house as easily as falling asleep.'

'The guards–?'

Larry incautiously shook his head and winced.

'Ouch! That hurt! There are no guards. That story is bunk. There probably were in Lane Leonard's time, but not now. I got in all right and I got out. More than half the containers are empty! I managed to get away from the park and I was within a few yards of my car when I was attacked; whoever it was must have spotted the car and waited for my return and I always thought I was clever – prided myself upon my wideness. I saw nobody, but I heard a sound and turned round, and probably that saved my life. Cosh!'

'You didn't see the man that hit you?'

'No, it was quite dark, but I'll know him

again, and he'll remember me for a long time. I carried a sword cane – one of those things you buy for a joke when you're in Spain and never expect to use. As I wasn't taking a gun because of my awful criminal record, I thought I'd be on the safe side and take that. Fortunately, I didn't lose hold of it, and before he could give me a second blow I gave him two slashes with it that made him yap and bolt. I couldn't see anything for blood, but I heard him smashing through a hedge. I don't know how I got back to the car and how I got to London.'

'May I ask,' said Mr Reeder,' exactly why you went to Sevenways?'

'She asked me to see her last night – asked me in French; and she asked me in French because she didn't want the chauffeur to hear her. That's when she told me she wanted to see you. Her room is on the park side of the house – it's called a castle, but it's a Tudor house really – three windows on the right from the portico. As I say, the window was barred, so my plan came unstuck.'

'What on earth were you going to do?' asked J.G.

'I was running away with her,' said Larry calmly. 'It was her idea.'

Mr Reeder was a picture of amazement.

'You were running away with her?' he said incredulously.

'That was the idea. She asked me to take her away. It sounds mad, but there it is. She must have trusted me, or she was desperate. I think a little of each.'

Mr Reeder went out to telephone, Larry protesting.

'Really, I don't want a doctor. A whack on the head is nothing.'

'A whack on the head that cuts four inches of skin and exposes the scalp is a very important matter,' said Mr Reeder, 'and I am one of the few remaining people who believe in doctors.'

A surgeon came in half an hour and did a little fancy stitching. Mr Reeder insisted that Larry should stay in the house; a very unusual request, for he never encouraged visitors, and this was the first guest he had had within the memory of his housekeeper.

It was early in the afternoon when Mr Reeder reached Sevenways Castle. It stood in an extensive park and, as Larry had said, there was very little about it that had the appearance of a castle. Its architecture was Tudor, except that on one end there stuck out a rather ugly, modern addition which was built, it seemed, of dressed stone and visible from the drive. This must be the treasure house, he thought.

He had telephoned the hour he expected to arrive, and Major Olbude was waiting for him under the porch. He led him into the panelled library, where a red fire glowed on an open hearth.

'I've been trying to make up my mind whether I should wait for you to arrive or whether I should send for the local police. Some ruffian attacked a gamekeeper of mine with a sword last night. I've had to send him away to London to be medically treated. Really, Mr Reeder, the events of the past few days have made me so nervous that I felt it prudent to send my niece to Paris. With one of my guards killed and my gamekeeper attacked, it almost looks as though there is some attempt being organised against the treasure house, and if I were not bound by the terms of the will I should send the whole contents of the place to the strongroom of a London bank. It is very disconcerting. By the way, you will be relieved to learn that I made a very careful inspection of the vault today, and none of the containers has been touched; all the seals are intact, as of course I expected they would be. I need hardly tell you that I am a little relieved, though there was no real cause for worrying. The strongroom is impregnable and, unless Buckingham was the most expert of thieves, he could not have forced the door without it being instantly detected. The key never leaves me day or night. I carry it, as a matter of fact, on a silver chain around my neck.'

'And none of the containers has been touched?' asked Mr Reeder.

'None. Would you like to see the vault?'

Mr Reeder followed him along the broad corridor of the castle into a little room which apparently was the major's study, and through a steel door, which he unlocked, into a small lobby, illuminated by a skylight heavily criss-crossed with steel bars. There was another steel door, and beyond this they came to a narrow stone passage which led to the treasure house proper.

It was a huge concrete and steel safe, placed within four walls. The only adjunct to the building was a small kitchenette, where the guards sat, and this was immediately opposite the steel door of the vault.

'I think we're entitled to call it a vault,' said the major, 'because it is sunk some five feet below the level on which we are present – one goes down steps to the interior–'

Mr Reeder was looking round.

'Where is the guard?' he asked.

The major spread out his hands, despair in his good-looking face.

'I'm afraid I lost my head, after what you told me. I dismissed them with a month's wages and packed them off the moment I came back. It was stupid of me, because I'm sure they are trustworthy, but once you've become suspicious of men in whom you've placed the greatest confidence, I think it is best to make a clean sweep.'

Mr Reeder examined the steel door carefully.

He saw, however, at a glance that only the most expert of bank-smashers could have forced his way into the treasure chamber, and then only with the aid of modern scientific instruments. It was certainly not a one-man job, and decidedly no task for an amateur.

He came back to the house, his hands thrust into his pockets, the inevitable umbrella hooked on his arm, his high-crowned hat on the back of his head. He stopped to admire one of the pieces of statuary which lined the broad hall.

'A very old house,' he said. 'I am interested in the manor houses of England.

Is there any possibility of looking over the place?'

Major Olbude hesitated.

'There's no reason why you shouldn't,' he said. 'Some of the rooms, of course, are locked up; in fact, we only use one wing.'

They went from room to room. The drawing room was empty. He saw on a low table a book. It was open in the middle, and lying face down on the table; a book that had been put aside by somebody who was so interested in the story that they were anxious to continue at the place they left off. Near by was a pair of reading glasses and a case. He made no comment, and went on to the dining room, with its Elizabethan panels and deep mullioned windows; stopped to admire the carved crest of the original owner of the building, and listened intently while Major Olbude told him the history of Sevenways.

'You don't wish to see upstairs?'

'I should rather like to. The old sleeping apartments in these manor houses have a singular interest for me. I am – um – something of a student of architecture,' said Mr Reeder untruthfully.

7

At the head of the grand stairway stretched a passage from which opened the principal bedrooms.

'This is my niece's room.'

He threw open a door and showed a rather gloomy-looking apartment with a four-poster bed.

'As I say, she went to Paris this morning–'

'And left everything very tidy,' murmured Mr Reeder. 'It's such a pleasure to find that trait in a young lady.'

There was no sign that the room had been lived in and there was a slight mustiness about it.

'There's little or nothing in this other wing, except my bedroom,' said the major, leading the way past the staircase.

He was walking more quickly, but Mr Reeder stopped opposite a doorway.

'There's one remark that was made by a Frenchman about an English manor house in the reign of Charles,' he said sententiously. 'Do you speak – er – French, Major?'

Now, the remarkable thing about Major Olbude was that he did not speak French. He had a knowledge of Greek and of Latin, but modern languages had never appealed to him, he said.

'His remark was this,' said Mr Reeder, and said something in French. He said it very loudly. *'If you are in the room, move your blind when you hear me talking outside the house.'*

'I'm afraid that is unintelligible to me,' said the major shortly.

'It means,' said Mr Reeder glibly, 'that the Englishman's idea of a good house is a comfortable bed inside a fortress. Now,' he said, as they went down the stairs together, 'I would like to see the house from the outside.'

They walked along the gravelled pathway running parallel with the front of the house. The major was growing obviously impatient; moreover, he was displaying a certain amount of anxiety, glancing round as though he were expecting an unwelcome visitor. Mr Reeder noticed these things.

When he came opposite the third window from the right of the porch, he said loudly, pointing to a distant clump of trees: 'Was it there your gamekeeper was attacked?'

As he spoke, he glanced quickly backwards. The white blind that covered the third window to the right of the porch moved slightly.

'No, it was in the opposite direction, on the other side of the house,' said the major shortly. 'Now would you like to see the sleeping quarters of Buckingham? The police have been here this morning – the Kentish police – and have made a thorough search, so I don't think it is worth while your examining the place. As far as I can gather, they found nothing.'

Mr Reeder looked at him thoughtfully.

'No, I don't think I want to see Buckingham's quarters, but there are one or two questions I would like to ask you. May I see the inside of the vault?'

'No, you may not.'

Olbude's voice was sharp, frankly unfriendly. He seemed to realise this, for he added almost apologetically: 'You see, Mr Reeder, I have a very heavy responsibility. This infernal trust is getting so much on my mind that I'm thinking of asking the courts to relive me of my guardianship.'

They were back in the library now. Mr Reeder was no longer the languid, charming and rather timid gentleman. He was the hectoring, domineering Mr Reeder, whom quite a number of people knew and disliked intensely.

'I want to see your niece,' he said.

'She's gone to Paris.'

'When did she go?'

'She went by car this morning.'

'Let me ask you one question; is your niece short-sighted? Does she wear glasses?'

Olbude was taken off his guard.

'Yes; the doctor ordered her to wear glasses for reading.'

'How many pairs of glasses has she?'

The major shrugged.

'What is the idea of these ridiculous questions?' he asked testily. 'So far as I know, she has one pair, a sort of blue-shaded tortoiseshell—'

'Then will you explain why she took a long journey and left behind her the book in which she was so interested, and her reading glasses? You will find them in the drawing room. I want to see her room.'

'I have shown you her room,' said Olbude, raising his voice.

'I want to see the third room from the left of the grand staircase.'

Olbude looked at him for a second, and laughed. 'My dear Mr Reeder, surely this is not the method of the Public Prosecutor's Department?'

'It is my method,' said Mr Reeder curtly.

There was a pause.

'I will go upstairs and get her,' said the major.

'If you don't mind, I will come with you.' Outside the door of the girl's room the major paused, key in hand.

'I will tell you the truth, though I don't see that this matter has anything to do with you,' he said. 'My niece has been very indiscreet. As far as I can gather, she made arrangements to run away with an unknown man, who, I have since ascertained, has a criminal record – you will be able to confirm this, for I understand you were in the case. Naturally, as her guardian, I have my duty to do, and as to my little fiction about her going to Paris–'

'Perhaps she will tell me all this herself,' said Reeder.

The major snapped back the key and threw open the door.

'Come out, Pamela, please. Mr Reeder wishes to see you.'

She came out into the light, her eyes upon her guardian.

'I think it is true, is it not, that you had made arrangements to leave this house, Pamela, and that because of this I locked you in your room?'

She nodded. The girl was terrified, was in

such fear that she could hardly stand. Yet, as Reeder sensed, it was not the major who inspired the fear.

'This is Mr Reeder; I think you met him yesterday. Mr Reeder seems to think there is something sinister in this act of discipline. Have I in any way ill-treated you?'

She shook her head, so slightly that the gesture was almost imperceptible.

'Is there anything you would like to say to Mr Reeder – any complaint you wish to make? Mr Reeder is a very important official in the Public Prosecutor's office.' There was a note of pomposity in his tone. 'You may be sure that if I have behaved in any way illegally, he will see that you are–'

'Quite unnecessary, isn't it, Major Olbude?' said Mr Reeder's quiet voice. 'I mean, all this – um – prompting and terrifying. Perhaps if I had a few minutes with the young lady in your library she might give me some information.'

'About what? You would like to ask her a few questions about me, would you?' asked Olbude.

'Curiously enough, I have come down here to investigate the murder of a man called Buckingham. If you are concerned in the murder of that man, I shall certainly ask

102

her questions about you.'

Reeder's eyes did not leave the man's face.

'If, on the other hand, that is a matter which does not concern you, the result of our conversation will be in no way embarrassing to you, Major Olbude. Did you know Buckingham, Miss Leonard?'

'Yes,' she said. Her voice was low and sweet. 'But not very well. I have seen him once or twice.'

'We had better go back to the library,' Olbude broke in; his voice was unsteady. 'I don't suppose this young lady can tell you very much that you want to know, but since you're intent on cross-examining her, there's no reason in the world why I should put obstacles in your way. Naturally, I haven't any desire that a young girl should discuss a beastly business like murder, but if that is the method of the Public Prosecutor's office, by all means go ahead with it.'

He took them back to the library, but made no attempt to leave them alone. Rather did he plant himself in the most comfortable chair in the room, within earshot.

She knew little about Buckingham. Mr Reeder could not escape the conviction that she was not terribly interested in that unfortunate man. She had seen the picture in the newspaper and had drawn her uncle's attention to the tragedy. She knew nothing of the treasure house, had only seen it from the outside, and had met none of the guards.

She was not overawed by Olbude's presence, but with every answer she gave to the detective's inquiries she cast a frightened glance towards the door as though she expected somebody would come in. Mr Reeder guessed who that somebody was.

He looked at his watch, and his attitude towards the girl suddenly changed. He had been gentle, almost grandmotherly with his 'um's' and 'er's', and now the hectoring Mr Reeder reappeared.

'I'm not quite satisfied with your answers, Miss Leonard,' he said, 'and I am going to take you up to Scotland Yard to question you still further.'

For a moment she was startled, looked at him in horror, and then she understood, and he saw the look of relief come into her eyes. The major had risen slowly to his feet.

'This is rather a high-handed proceeding,' he quavered, 'and I think I can save you a lot of trouble. I'll make a confession to you, Mr Reeder; I have been shielding this man Buckingham. Why I should do so, heaven only knows, except that I didn't wish to incur undesirable publicity for my niece. When I visited the treasure house this morning I found that four of the containers were empty. You asked me if you might see the vault, and I refused. I think it was stupid of me; and now, if you wish, I can throw a great deal of light, not only upon the robbery, but upon the disappearance of this wretched man–'

'Let me tell you something,' said Reeder. 'It is an old story, part of which was told me by a boy from your school, and part I have unearthed in my own way.'

The major licked his dry lips.

'It is a story about a namesake of yours,' Reeder went on, 'a rather clever man, who had a commission in the Territorial Army. He was, in fact, of your rank, and if I remember rightly, his Christian name was – um – Digby.'

He saw the colour fade from Olbude's face and heard his quick breathing.

'He was, unhappily, a victim of the narcotic habit,' said Mr Reeder, not taking his eyes from the man's face, 'and I will do him this justice, that he was heartily ashamed of his weakness and when he sank, as he did sink, to the level of a peddler of cocaine, he took another name. I was responsible for his arrest, with several other people engaged in that beastly traffic; and to me he confided that he had very rich relations who might help him. He even mentioned the name of a brother-in-law named Lane Leonard. At this time he had reached, as I say, a pretty low level. I am not a philanthropist, but I have a weakness for helping the hopeless, and the more hopeless they are – such is my peculiar – um – perversity – the more I endeavour to produce miracles. I rarely succeed. I did not succeed with Major Digby Olbude. I kept in touch with him after he came out of prison, but he managed to drift away beyond my reach, and I did not hear of him again till I learned that he had died in St Pancras Infirmary. He was buried in the name of Smith, but, unhappily for everybody concerned, there was an old acquaintance of his in the hospital at the same time, and this old acquaintance formed the link by which Lidgett was able to trace this unfortunate man.'

Olbude found his voice.

'There are quite a large number of Olbudes in the world,' he said, 'and Digby is a family name. He may have been a connection of mine.'

'I don't think he was any relation of yours,' said Mr Reeder gently. 'I think I had better see Lidgett, and then I would like to telephone to Scotland Yard and bring down the officer in charge of the Buckingham case. I'm afraid it is going to be a rather unpleasant experience for you, my friend.'

'I know nothing about Buckingham,' said the man huskily. 'I had little to do with the guards. I saw them and paid them, and that is all.'

'When you say "guards" you mean "guard",' said Mr Reeder. 'There have been no keepers of the treasure house since shortly after Mr Lane Leonard's death, the only man employed being Buckingham. It only needed the most elementary of inquiries to dispose of that absurd story. You have the key of the treasure house, by the way?'

The other shook his head.

'Suspended round your neck by a silver chain?' suggested Mr Reeder.

'No,' said Olbude brusquely. 'I have never had it. Lidgett has it.'

Mr Reeder smiled.

'Then there is all the more reason for interviewing that enterprising chauffeur,' he said.

Pamela had stood silent through this exchange. There were significant gaps which she could fill.

'Lidgett is in his room,' said Olbude at last. 'I suppose it's going to be very serious for me?'

'I'm afraid it is,' said Reeder.

The man bit his lip and stared out of the window.

'Nothing can be very much worse than the humiliating life I have lived for the past few years,' he said. 'I never dreamt that money and wealth could be purchased at such a ghastly price.'

He looked at the girl with a quizzical smile.

'In this precious treasure house there is very nearly five hundred thousand pounds,' he said. 'I made a rough survey the other morning. Lidgett was kind enough to let me have the keys – in fact, he had to allow this, because I flatly refused to make any statement concerning the condition of the Treasury until he let me satisfy myself that the money was not entirely gone.

'He and Buckingham were fellow gamblers. I've never quite known how Buckingham came into his confidence, but I have a fancy that Buckingham was necessary for the transport of the gold. I will say this, that I was not aware that the money was being stolen, although I confess I was a little suspicious. When I taxed Lidgett with plundering the treasure house he very frankly admitted the fact, and defied me to take any action against him.

'I know they quarrelled a great deal, and, as Miss Lane Leonard will tell you, there was some fighting in which Lidgett got the worst of it. The murder was probably subsequent to this. And now I think I had better call Lidgett.'

He went out of the room and up the stairs, past the far end of the left wing and knocked at the door. A surly voice asked who was there, and when he replied he heard the shuffle of slippered feet across the bare floor and the key was turned in the lock.

Lidgett was in a dressing gown, his face covered with sticking plaster.

'Has he gone?' he growled.

Major Oldbude shook his head, a smile on his good-looking face.

'No,' he said lightly. 'At the moment he is in the library with Miss Lane Leonard.'

Lidgett gaped at him.

'With her? Talking to her? What the hell's the idea?'

'The idea is that I have told Mr Reeder as much of the truth as I know. I naturally couldn't tell him exactly the circumstances leading to the murder of Buckingham, because I don't know what preceded it. I gather from your activity in the garage the next day, and the amount of washing down you did, that the murder was committed in the garage. I know you burnt clothes in the furnace, but all this is quite unimportant.'

Lidgett stood, speechless. And then, as he realised all that was implied: 'You swine!' he screamed.

Mr Reeder heard two quick shots and then a third. He flew up the stairs, arriving simultaneously with a manservant. When he came back to the girl his face was grave.

'I'm going to take you up to London, young lady' he said. 'I have asked one of the maids to pack your things and bring them down.'

'I can go up–' she began.

'There is no need.'

'What has happened?' she asked.

'We'll talk about it in the car,' said Reeder.

In truth he did nothing of the sort. He did not even tell her that the key attached to a silver chain, which he carried in his pocket, had been taken from the neck of the dead

Lidgett and was still spotted with his blood.

'The story, so far as I can piece it together,' said Mr Reeder to his chief, 'is somewhat complicated, but is not by any means as complicated as it appeared. Which, sir, is a peculiarity of most human stories.

'The real Major Olbude was a drug addict who died in St Pancras Infirmary. He was a relative of Lane Leonard's, and at one time there had been certain business associations between them. When Lane Leonard found he was approaching his end, his mind went back to this brother-in-law and he sent Lidgett in search of him. By a stroke of luck Lidgett was able to trace Olbude, and discovered that he had died at St Pancras Infirmary and been buried under the name of Smith.

'You must realise that Lidgett was a very shrewd and possibly a clever fellow. He was certainly cunning. He knew that unless a guardian were produced the estate would be thrown into Chancery and he would lose his employment, for he had never been a favourite with Miss Pamela. He conceived the idea of producing a spurious Major Olbude, and his choice fell upon a man he had met at a gambling house in Dean

Street, a rather pompous schoolmaster who had this unfortunate failing, and was in the habit of coming to London every weekend to play at the club.

'Mr Tasbitt was a master at Fernleigh College, a public school at which Larry O'Ryan was a scholar and from which he was expelled. There is no doubt whatever that the boy was innocent, and that the real thief was this same Tasbitt. Depending upon his master's failing senses, Lidgett took Tasbitt, who probably agreed to fraud with the greatest reluctance and in some terror, to Sevenways Castle. Tasbitt was introduced and accepted as Olbude; there was very little risk; few people knew Olbude. I have only today learned that his title of major was a piece of vanity on his part, and that he had only served some twelve months in the Territorial Army and had not risen beyond the rank of second lieutenant. But that is by the way.

'All might have gone well if Buckingham and Lidgett had not quarrelled, probably over the division of the loot. The two men were running a land development company, and though this was not very successful it was by no means a failure. I have now been able to trace Lidgett's account, and a very considerable portion of the missing money will be in time restored to its owner when certain properties are liquidated.

'It was unfortunate for Tasbitt that O'Ryan was in the vicinity of my office the day he called on me, for he was instantly recognised and, as it appeared, the recognition was mutual.'

When the Assistant Public Prosecutor heard the story he asked a pertinent question.

'Will this young lady marry O'Ryan?'

Mr Reeder nodded.

'I think so,' he said gravely.

'Isn't there a possibility that he's after her money?'

Mr Reeder shook his head.

'He has quite a lot of money of his own,' he said, a little regretfully.

THE SHADOW MAN

1

When Mr Reeder went to New York in connection with the Gessler Bank fraud he was treated as though he were a popular member of a royal family. New York policemen, who are more accustomed to seeing humanity in all sorts of odd shapes and appearances, and with that innate politeness and hospitality which is theirs, saw nothing amusing in the old-fashioned coat, which he kept tightly buttoned, in his square hat, or even his side-whiskers. They offered him the respect which was due to a very great detective. They were less deceived by his seeming timidity and his preference for everybody's opinion but his own than were their English colleagues.

His stay was a comparatively short one, yet, in the time at his disposal, he glided through the police headquarters of four great American cities, saw Atlanta prison, and, two days before he sailed, travelled by

115

train to Ossning, passed through the steel gates of Sing-Sing and inspected that very interesting building under the guidance of the Deputy Warden, from card index to death house.

'There's one man I'd have liked you to see,' said the Deputy Warden just before they parted. 'He's an Englishman – he's called Redsack. Have you ever heard of him?'

Mr Reeder shook his head.

'There are so many people I've never heard of,' he murmured apologetically, 'and Mr Redsack is one of them. Is he staying here – er – for a long time?'

'Life,' said the other laconically, 'and he's lucky to escape the chair. He's broken three prisons, but he won't break Sing-Sing – the most dangerous man we have in this institution.'

Mr Reeder rubbed his chin thoughtfully.

'I – um – would like to have seen him,' he said.

The Deputy Warden smiled.

'Just now he's not visible, but he'll be out tomorrow,' he said. 'We had to put him in a punishment cell for trying to escape. I thought you might know him. He's had four convictions in the United States, and he's probably guilty of more murders than any prisoner inside these walls; he certainly has the biggest brain I've met with since I first dealt with criminals.'

Mr Reeder smiled sadly and shook his head.

'I have never yet met – um – anything that resembled a brain in the criminal world,' he said, with a deep melancholy. 'Redsack? What a pity his crimes were not committed in England.'

'Why?' asked the Deputy Warden, in surprise.

'He would be dead by now,' said Mr Reeder, and heaved a deep sigh.

The departure of Mr Reeder's ship was delayed twenty-four hours, and he filled in the time very profitably by gluing himself to the record department at Police Head-quarters, New York, and making himself acquainted with Mr Redsack.

Redsack was a consistently elusive person. There was no photograph of him that had not been cleverly distorted by his own facial manoeuvres. It was not true to say that he was an Englishman; he had been born in Vancouver and had been educated in London; and at thirty had a record that would have made him respected in any criminal circle and nowhere else. Almost Mr Reeder, albeit reluctantly, agreed with the Deputy Warden that this man showed evidence of genius. He was clever, he was ruthless. In the bare police records, and even without the assistance of an explanatory dossier, the investigator noticed three samples of the operation of a brilliant mind.

Mr Reeder sailed at midnight on the following day. As, clad in his gay pyjamas, he climbed into his bed, he could have no idea that, five decks below him, working in the galley, was the man he had left in the punishment cell at Sing-Sing and, oddly enough, there was nothing in the newspapers about this astonishing fact.

When the Deputy Warden had said again at parting, a little regretfully: 'Pity you can't see Redsack. He'll be out tomorrow,' he was unconsciously a prophet.

It was the most daring and the most sensational escape that Sing-Sing had known. It happened on a dull, wintry afternoon, when a dozen prisoners were at their exercises in the big yard of the old prison. They were watching, with some curiosity and interest, the manoeuvres of a balloon which, caught in a half-gale, was tacking over the Hudson in a vain effort to get back on its course. Ballooning was an unusual sport. Suddenly, without warning, something seemed to go wrong, and the big gasbag, sagging in the middle, began to make a rapid and oblique descent. Its trail rope came over the wall of the prison yard, dragging along the ground and the nearest man to it seized it. As he did so, a heavy quantity of ballast was released from the gondola beneath the bag, and the balloon shot up, carrying with it a Mr Redsack.

The guards saw their charge carried over their heads, and could neither fire at him nor do anything but watch helplessly.

The airship drifted across the Hudson into New Jersey, came low again.

Mr Redsack dropped. It was near a small village. Conveniently close at hand, standing unattended by the side of the road, was a dilapidated car and on the back seat a suitcase. Nobody seemed to have witnessed his surprising descent but he drove for twenty minutes before stopping the car and changing into the clothes from the suitcase. He put the prison uniform in the empty case and left it in a convenient wood.

Near the outskirts of Jersey City, he abandoned the car, walked towards the city and boarded a bus. He came by ferry to New York and eventually to the quay where the outward mail was waiting. After that everything was very simple for Mr Redsack.

Galley hands were scarce and money is an eloquent letter of recommendation. He had been assigned his watch, and was peeling potatoes with the greatest industry before the ship pulled out of New York harbour.

If you had told Mr Reeder it was a coincidence that he should at this stage have been brought into contact with one of the most remarkable criminals of our time, he would have shaken his head half-heartedly and in the most apologetic terms have differed from you.

'It is no coincidence – um – that any detective should meet, or nearly meet, any criminal, any more than it is a coincidence that the glass of water you are – er – drinking should at some time or other have been part of the Atlantic Ocean.'

When the people in Scotland Yard speculate upon this peculiar happening they always begin with the word 'if'. 'If' Redsack had not been in the punishment cell; 'if' Mr Reeder had only seen him... Quite a lot of trouble might have been saved, and the L and O Bank was by no means the beginning or the end of it.

That Mr Reeder forgot about Redsack is unlikely. When he reached England and went through the files the man's name was familiar. It was inevitable that his record should go down in an abbreviated form in his casebook, for Mr Reeder despised the story of no criminal, and held the view that crime, like art, knew no frontiers.

But, strangely enough, the name of Redsack did not occur to the man from Whitehall in connection with the L and O Bank affair.

2

Mr Reeder very seldom went to the theatre. When he did he preferred the strong and romantic drama to the more subtle problem plays which are so popular with the leisured classes.

He went to see *Killing Time,* and was a little disappointed, for he detected 'the man who did it' in the first act, and thereafter the play ceased to have any great interest for him.

The unpleasant happening of the evening occurred between the first and second acts, when Mr Reeder was pacing the vestibule, smoking one of his cheap cigarettes, and speculating upon the advisability of recovering his coat and hat from the cloakroom and escaping after the interval bell had rung and the audience had gone back into the auditorium.

There approached him a resplendent man. He was stout, rather tall, very florid. He wore a perpetual smile, which was made up of nine-tenths of amused contempt. His stubby nails were manicured and polished; Mr Reeder suspected that they were faintly tinted. His clothes fitted him all too perfectly, and when he smiled his way up to Mr Reeder that gentleman had a feeling that he would like to go back and see the second act after all.

'You're Mr Reeder, aren't you?' he said in a tone which challenged denial. 'My name is Hallaty, Gunnersbury branch of the L and O Bank. You came down to see me one day about a fellow who'd been passing dud cheques.'

Mr Reeder fixed his glasses on the end of his nose and looked over them at his new acquaintance.

'Yes, I – um – remember there was a branch of the bank at Gunnersbury,' he said. 'Very interesting how these branches are spreading.'

'It's rather funny to see you here at a theatre,' smiled Mr Hallaty.

'I – um – suppose it is,' said Mr Reeder.

'It's a funny thing,' the loquacious man went on, 'I was talking to a friend of mine, Lord Lintil – you may have met him. I know him personally; in fact, we're quite pals.'

Mr Reeder was impressed.

'Really?' he said respectfully. 'I haven't

seen Lord Lintil since his third bankruptcy. Quite an interesting man.'

Mr Hallaty was jarred but not shaken.

'Misfortune comes to everybody, even to the landed gentry,' he said, a little sternly.

'You were talking to him about me?'

Mr Reeder spared himself the admonition which was coming.

'And – um – what did you say about me?'

For a moment the Manager of the Gunnersbury branch did not seem inclined to pursue his aristocratic reminiscences.

'I was saying how clever you were.'

Mr Reeder wriggled unhappily.

'We were talking about these bank frauds that are going on, and how impossible it is to bring the – what do you call 'ems – perpetrators to justice, eh? That's what we want to do, Mr Reeder – bring 'em to justice.'

His pale eyes never left Mr Reeder's.

'A most admirable idea,' agreed the detective.

He wondered if any helpful advice was likely to be forthcoming.

'I suppose there must be a system by which you can stop this sort of thing going on.'

'I'm sure there must be,' said Mr Reeder.

He looked at his watch and shook his head.

'I am quite anxious to see the second act,' he said untruthfully.

'Personally,' Mr Hallaty went on with the greatest complacency, 'I'd like to be put in charge of one of these cases, on the basis of the old and well-known saying of which you've no doubt heard.'

Mr Reeder when he was most innocent was most malignant. He was innocent now.

'"Set a thief to catch a thief"? But surely not, Mr – I didn't quite catch your name?'

The man went purple.

'What I mean was *Quis custodiet ipsos custodes?* – a Latin proverb,' he said loudly.

Fortunately the bell rang at that moment and Mr Reeder made his escape. But it was only temporary. When he got outside the theatre that night, after the conclusion of the third and tamest act of the play, he found his banking friend waiting.

'I wondered if you'd like to come up to my club and have a drink?'

Mr Reeder shook his head.

'It is delightful of you, Mr – um–'

Mr Hallaty told him his name for the third time.

'But I never go to clubs and I do not drink

126

anything stronger than barley water.'

'Can I drop you anywhere?' asked Mr Hallaty.

Mr Reeder said he was walking and therefore could not be dropped.

'But I thought you lived at Brockley?'

'I walk there,' said Mr Reeder. 'I find it so good for my complexion.'

He was not unduly surprised at the persistence of this very self-satisfied man. Quite a number of people did their best to scrape acquaintance with the country's greatest authority on crime against banks; some out of morbid curiosity, some for more personal reasons, some who gave him an importance which perhaps he did not deserve, and desired to share it even to the smallest extent.

Mr Hallaty was a type, self-important, pompous, self-sufficient and quite self-satisfied. To Mr Reeder's annoyance a few days later, when he was eating his bun and drinking his glass of milk at a teashop, the smiling man appeared before him and sat down at the same table. Mr Reeder's bun was hardly nibbled, his milk remained untouched. There was no escape. He sat in silence, listening to Mr Hallaty's views on crime, the detection of crime, banking methods and their inadequacy, but mainly about Mr Hallaty's extraordinary genius, prescience and shrewdness.

'They'd be very clever to get past me, whether they're crooks or whether they're straight,' said Mr Hallaty.

He lit a small and disagreeable cigar. Mr Reeder looked significantly at a sign which said 'No Smoking.'

'You don't mind, do you?' asked Hallaty.

'Very much,' said Mr Reeder, and the other man laughed as though it were the best joke in the world, and went on smoking.

'Personally,' he said, 'I think professional crooks are not clever. They think they are, but when they're matched against the intelligence of the average businessman, or a man a little above the average, they're finished.'

He chatted on in this vein until Mr Reeder put down his bun, glared solemnly over his half-glass of milk, and said, with startling distinctness: 'Will you please go away? I want to have my lunch.' Thick-skinned as the man was, he was taken aback; went very red, apologised incoherently, and swaggered out of the shop without paying the bill for his cup of tea. Mr Reeder paid it gratefully.

Recalling those two conversations, Mr Reeder remembered later that most of the inquiries which the Bank Manager made had to do with systems of search for missing delinquents. When he got home that night he very carefully marked down the name of Mr Hallaty in a little book the cover of which was inscribed with a big question mark.

Yet it seemed impossible to believe that a man who was so aggressive could be anything but an honest man. Men engaged in the tiresome trade of roguery are suave men, polite men. They soothe and please – it is part of their stock in trade. Only the twenty shillings to the pound and look-the-whole-world-in-the-face man could afford to be boorish. And Mr Hallaty was undoubtedly boorish.

He was, as he claimed, the Manager of the Gunnersbury branch of the London and Orient Bank, and was a man of style and importance. He had a flat in Albemarle Street, drove his own car, had a chauffeur, a valet and quite a nice circle of reliable friends. He had also a very humble flat in Hammersmith, and this was his official address.

The Gunnersbury branch of the L and O

was in its way rather important. It carried the accounts of half a dozen big plants on the Great West Road, The Kelson Gas Works, and the Brite-Lites Manufacturing Corporation, and was therefore responsible for very heavy payrolls.

About a month after the teashop talk Mr Hallaty called at the London office of the Ninth Avenue Bank on Lombard Street, and said that he had had a request from the most important of his customers for a large supply of American currency. The customer in question was an Anglo-American concern, and in order to celebrate some new amalgamation the directors had decided to pay a big bonus in dollars. Could the Ninth Avenue Bank supply the necessary greenbacks – fifty-seven thousand dollars, no less?

The American bank, after the way of American banks, was obliging. It undertook to sell dollars to the required amount, and on the Friday afternoon at two o'clock Hallaty called and exchanged English currency for American.

At the headquarters of the L and O Bank there was rather an urgent conference of general and assistant general managers that afternoon.

'I'm worried about this man Hallaty,' said

the chief. 'One of our secret service people has discovered that he is living at the rate of ten thousand a year.'

'What is his salary?' somebody asked.

'Two thousand five hundred.'

There was a little silence.

'He is a very careful man,' said one. 'He may have some very good investments.'

The question became instantly urgent, for at that moment came an official with a telephone message from yet another American bank – the Dyers Bank of New York. Mr Hallaty had just purchased a hundred thousand dollars' worth of American currency. He had negotiated the purchase in the morning, giving as a reason the requirements of the Brite-Lite Corporation. The Dyers Bank had certain misgivings after the departure of Mr Hallaty with a thousand notes for one hundred dollars tucked away in a briefcase, and those misgivings were caused by a glimpse which one of the commissionaires had of the contents of the briefcase – already half-full of American notes.

The bank detectives sped to Gunnersbury – Mr Hallaty was not there. He had the key of the vault, but the detectives had taken with them a duplicate key from the safe at the head office.

There should have been, in preparation for the next day's pay-out, some £72,000 in the vaults. In point of fact, there were a few odd bundles of ten-shilling and pound notes.

Mr Hallaty was not at the flat where he was supposed to live, nor at the flat in Albemarle Street, where he actually lived. His valet was there, and his chauffeur.

The Axford airport had a clue to give. Mr Hallaty had arrived that afternoon, seemingly with the intention of flying the small aeroplane which he kept there. He was well known as an amateur flyer and was a skilled pilot. When the aeroplane was removed from the hangar it was discovered that the wings had been slashed and other damage done which made the machine unusable. How it had happened was a mystery which nobody could explain.

Mr Hallaty, on seeing the damage, had turned deathly pale and had re-entered his car and driven away, carrying with him his two suitcases.

From that moment Mr Hallaty was not seen. He vanished into London and was lost.

If the losses to the bank had been £72,000 only, it would have been serious enough.

Unfortunately, Hallaty was a very ingenious man, with a very complete knowledge of the English banking system. When accounts came in and were checked, when the clearing-house made its quick report and certain northern and midland banking branches presented their claims, it was found that considerably over a quarter of a million of money had vanished.

There was much to admire here in the way of perfect training and clever expedient, but the L and O directors were not sufficiently broad-minded to offer any testimonial to their missing Manager.

Three days after he had vanished, Mr Reeder came upon the scene. He was in his most apologetic mood. He apologised for being called in three days after he should have been called in; he apologised to the gloomy Chairman for the offence of his unfaithful servant; he apologised for being wet (he carried a furled umbrella on his arm) and by inference regretted his side-whiskers, his hat and his tightly-fitting coat.

The Chairman, by some odd process of mind, felt that a considerable amount of responsibility had been lifted from his shoulders.

'Now, Mr Reeder, you see exactly what

133

has happened, and the bank is leaving everything in your hands. Perhaps it would have been wiser if we'd called you in before.'

Mr Reeder plucked up spirit to say that he thought it might have been.

'Here are the reports,' said the General Manager, pushing a folder full of large, imposing manuscript sheets. 'The police have not the slightest idea where he's gone to, and I confess that I never expect to see Hallaty or the money again.'

Mr Reeder scratched his chin.

'It would be improper in me if I said that I hope I never do,' he sighed. 'It's the Tynedale case all over again, and the Manchester and Oldham Bank case, and the South Devon Bank case – in fact – um – there is here the evidence of a system, sir, if I may venture to suggest such a thing.'

The General Manager frowned.

'A system? You mean all these offences against the banks you have mentioned are organised?'

Mr Reeder nodded.

'I think so, sir,' he said gently. 'If you will compare one with the other you will discover, I think, that in every case the Manager has, on one pretext or another, converted large sums of English currency into francs or dollars, that his last operation has been in London, and that he has vanished when the discovery of his defalcations has been made.'

The General Manager shivered, for Reeder was presenting to him the ogre of the banking world – the organised conspirator. Only those who understand banking know just what this means.

'I hadn't noticed that,' he said; 'but un-doubtedly it is a fact.'

3

Other people had observed these sinister happenings. A bankers' association summoned an urgent meeting, and Mr Reeder, an authority upon bank crimes, was called into consultation. In such moments as these Reeder was very practical, not at all vague. Rather was he definite – and when Mr Reeder was definite he was blood-curdling. He came to a sensational point after a very diffident beginning.

'There are some things – er – gentlemen, to which I am loath to give the authority of my support. Theories which – um – belong to the more sensational press and certainly to no scientific system. Yet I must tell you, gentlemen, that in my opinion we are for the first time face to face with an organized attempt to rob the banks on the grand scale.'

The president of the association looked at him incredulously.

'You don't mean to suggest, Mr Reeder, that there is a definite co-ordination between these various frauds?'

Mr Reeder nodded solemnly.

'They have that appearance. I would not care to give a definite opinion one way or the other, but I certainly would not rule that out.'

One member of the association shook his white head.

'There are such things as crimes of imitation, Mr Reeder. When some man steals money in a peculiar way, other weak-minded individuals follows suit.'

Mr Reeder smiled broadly.

'I'm afraid that won't do, sir,' he said with the greatest kindness. 'You speak as though the details of the fraud had been published. In three cases out of five the general public know nothing about these crimes. In no case have the particulars been published or have they been available even to the managers of branch banks. And yet in every case the crime has followed along exactly similar lines. In every case there has been a man, holding a responsible position in the bank, who, through gambling on the Stock Exchange or for some other reason or from habits of extravagance, has – I will not say been compelled to rob the bank, because a man is quite – um – a free agent in such matters, but has certainly succeeded in relieving your – er – various institutions of very considerable sums of money. These are the points I make.'

He ticked them off on his fingers.

'First of all, a manager or assistant manager in straitened circumstances. Secondly, a very carefully organised plan to draw, upon one given day, the maximum sum of money which can be drawn from headquarters, the changing over of the money into foreign currency, and the complete disappearance of the bank manager, all within twenty-four hours. It is an unusual kind of fraud, for it does not involve of itself any false bookkeeping. In several cases we have found that a petty fraud, in comparison with the greater offence, has been going on for some time and has been obviously the cause of the greater crime. Gentlemen' – Mr Reeder's voice was serious – 'there is something very big in the way of criminal activity in London, and an organisation is in existence which is not only directing these frauds and profiting by them, but is offering to the men who commit them asylum during their stay here and facilities for getting out of the country without detection. I'm going to deal with the situation from this angle, and my only chance of putting a stop to it is if I am able to catch one of the minor criminals immediately before he brings off the big coup. I want from every bank a list of all their suspected staff, and I want this list before the bank inspectors go in to examine the books, and certainly before anything like an arrest is made.'

Instructions to this effect were immediately issued, and the very next morning Mr Reeder had before him in his bureau at the Public Prosecutor's office a list of bank officials against whom there was a question mark. It was a very small list, representing a microscopic percentage of the enormous staffs employed in the business of banking. One man had been betting heavily, and attached to his name was a list of his bookmakers and what, to Mr Reeder, was more important, exact details as to the period of time his betting operations covered.

Reeder's pencil went slowly down the list until it stopped before the name of L.G.H Reigate. Mr Reigate was twenty-eight, and an assistant branch manager, and his 'offence' was that he had been engaged in real estate speculation, had bought on a rising market, and for some time past had vainly endeavoured to get rid of his holdings. His salary was £1,500 a year; he lived with a half-sister in a small flat at Hampstead. He had apparently no other vices, spent most of his evenings at home, did not drink and was a light smoker.

The reports were very thorough. There was not a detail which Mr Reeder did not examine with the greatest care, for on these minor details often hang great issues.

He went through the remaining list and came back to Mr Reigate. Evidently here there was a case which might repay his private and personal investigation. He jotted down the address on a scrap of paper and made a few inquiries in the City. They were entirely satisfactory, for on the third probe he found a Canadian bank which had been asked if it could supply Canadian dollars in exchange for sterling, and if the maximum amount could be so supplied on any average day. The inquiry had come not from this branch, but from a client of the branch. Reeder spread his feelers a little wider, and stumbled on a second inquiry from the same client. He went to the general manager of the head office. Mr Reigate was known as a very conscientious young man and, except for the fact that he had been engaged in real estate speculation, the exact extent of which was unknown, there were no marks, black or red, against him.

'Who is the Branch Manager?' asked Mr Reeder, and was told.

The gentleman in question was a very reliable man, though inclined to be impetuous.

'He is a most excellent fellow, but loses his head at times. As he always loses it on the side of the bank we have no serious complaints against him.'

The name of the manager was Wallat, and that week a strange thing happened to him. He received a letter from a man whose name he did not remember, but who had apparently been an old customer of the bank.

'I wonder if you would care to take a fortnight's trip to the fjords on a luxury ship? A client of ours has booked two passages but is unable to go, and has asked me to present the passages to any friend of mine who may wish to make the trip. As you were so good to me in the past – I don't suppose you remember the circumstances or even recall my name – I shall be glad to pass them on to you.'

Now, the curious thing was that only a week before the Manager had spoken enviously of a friend of his who was making that very trip. He had always wanted to see Norway and the beauties of Scandinavia, and here out of the blue came an unrivalled opportunity.

His vacation was due; he immediately put in a request to headquarters for leave. The request went before the Assistant General Manager and was granted. The boat was due to leave on the Thursday night, but on Tuesday the Manager, in a burst of zeal, decided to make a rough examination of certain books.

What he found there put all ideas of holiday out of his mined. On the Wednesday morning he called before him Mr Reigate, and the pale-faced young man listened with growing terror to a recital of the irregularities which had been discovered. At this sign of his guilt the Manager, true to his tradition, lost his head, threatened a prosecution and, in a moment of hysteria, sent for a policeman. It was an irregular act, for prosecutions are initiated by the directors.

Panic engendered panic; Reigate put on his hat, walked from the bank, and was immediately pursued by a bareheaded Manager. The young man, in blind terror, leapt on the back of an ambulance which happened to be passing, and was immediately dragged off by a policeman who had joined in the pursuit. If the Manager had only kept his head the matter could have been corrected. As it was, he charged his assistant with the defalcations. Reigate admitted them and was put into a cell.

Bank headquarters were furious. They had been committed to a prosecution, and, as a sequel, the possibility of an action for damages. Mr Reeder was called in at once, and went into consultation with the bank's solicitors. He interviewed the young man, and found him incoherent with terror and quite incapable of giving any information. The next morning he was brought before a magistrate and remanded.

Apparently the magistrate took a serious view, for although Reigate, who was now a little calmer, asked for bail, that bail was put at a prohibitive sum. The young man was taken to prison.

That afternoon, however, there appeared

before the magistrate Sir George Polkley, who offered himself as surety. The name apparently was a famous one. Sir George was a well-known north country ship-builder. He was accompanied at the police court by a gentleman who gave the name of an eminent firm of Newcastle solicitors. The surety was accepted, and Reigate was released from Brixton prison that after-noon.

At seven o'clock that night Scotland Yard rang up Mr Reeder.

'You know Reigate was bailed out this afternoon?'

'Yes, I saw it in the newspapers,' said Mr Reeder. 'Sir George Polkley stood surety – how on earth did he know Sir George?'

'We've just had a wire from Polkley's solicitors in Newcastle. They know nothing whatever about it. Sir George is in the south of France, and his solicitors have sent nobody to London to represent them. What is more, they have never heard of Reigate.'

Mr Reeder, lounging in his chair, sat bolt upright.

'Then the bail was a fake? Where is Reigate?'

'He can't be found. He drove away from Brixton in a taxi, accompanied by the alleged solicitor, and he has not been seen since.'

Here was a problem for Mr Reeder, and one after his own heart. Who had gone to all that trouble to get Reigate released – and why? His frauds, if they were provable, did not involve more than three or four hundred pounds. Who wanted him released on bail – immediately released? There was no question at all that, high as the bail was, the necessary sureties would have been forthcoming in twenty-four hours. But somebody was very anxious to get Reigate out of prison with the least possible delay.

Mr Reeder interviewed the Public Prosecutor.

'It's all very, very odd,' he said, running his fingers through his thin hair. 'I suppose it is susceptible of a very simple explanation, but unfortunately I've got the mind of a criminal.'

The Public Prosecutor smiled.

'And how does your criminal mind interpret this happening?' he asked.

Mr Reeder shook his head.

'Rather badly, I'm afraid. I – um – should not like to be Mr Reigate!'

He had sent for the cowed and agitated Manager. He was a pompous little man, rotund of figure and round in face, and he perspired very easily. For half an hour he sat on the edge of a chair, facing Mr Reeder, and he spent most of that half-hour mopping his brow and his neck with a large white handkerchief.

'Headquarters have been most unkind to me, Mr Reeder,' he quavered. 'After all the years of faithful service... The worst they can say about me is that I was misled through my zeal for the bank. I suppose it was wrong of me to have this young man arrested, but I was so shocked, so – if I may use the expression – devastated.'

'Yes, I'm sure,' murmured Mr Reeder. 'You were going on vacation, you tell me? That is news to me.'

It was now that he learned for the first time about the two passages for the fjords. Fortunately the Manager had the letter with him. Mr Reeder read it quickly, reached for his telephone and put through an inquiry.

'I seem to remember the address,' he said as he hung up the 'phone. 'It has a familiar sound to it. I think you will find it is an accommodation address, and the gentleman who wrote to you has in fact no existence.'

'But he sent the tickets! They're made out in my name,' said the Manager triumphantly, and then his face fell. 'I shan't be able to go now, of course.'

Mr Reeder looked at him, and in his eyes there was pained reproach.

'I'm afraid you won't be able to go now, and I'm quite satisfied in my mind that you would have been very sorry if you had gone! Those tickets were intended to serve one purpose – to get you out of the bank and out of England, and to give young Mr Reigate an opportunity of bringing home the beans – if you'll excuse the vulgarity.'

Mr Reeder was both puzzled and enlightened. Here was another typical bank case, planned on exactly the same lines as the others, and revealing, beyond any question of doubt, the operation of a mastermind.

As soon as he got rid of the Bank Manager he took a cab and drove to Hampstead. Miss Jean Reigate had just returned from work when he arrived. She had read of her brother's misfortune in the evening newspaper on her way back from her office, and it struck Mr Reeder that she was not as agitated by the news as the world would expect her to be. She was a pretty girl, a slim brunette, and looked much younger than her twenty-four years.

'I haven't heard from my brother,' she

said. 'He's really my half-brother, but we've been very great friends all our lives, and I'm terribly upset about all this.'

She crossed to the window and looked out. Mr Reeder thought that she was not a young lady who very readily showed her feelings. She was obviously exercising great self-control now. Her lips were pressed closely together; her eyes were filled with unshed tears, and he sensed rather than observed the tension she was enduring.

Suddenly she turned.

'I'll tell you, Mr Reeder.'

She saw his eyebrows go up and smiled faintly.

'Oh, yes, I realise you haven't told me your name, but I know you. You're quite famous in the City.'

Mr Reeder was covered in genuine confusion, but came instantly to business when she hesitated.

'Well, what are you going to tell me?' he asked gently.

'I'm almost relieved. That is what I was going to say. I've been expecting something to happen for a long time. Johnny hasn't been himself; he's been terribly worried over his land deals, and I know he's been short of cash – in fact, I lent him a hundred pounds last month. But I thought he'd got over the worst because he returned the money the following week – in fact much more than the money; five hundred dollars is worth nearly two hundred pounds.'

'Dollars?' said Mr Reeder sharply. 'Did he repay you in dollars?'

She nodded.

'In dollar bills?'

'Yes, five bills of a hundred dollars. I put them in my bank.'

Mr Reeder was now very alert.

'Where did he get them?' he asked.

She shook her head.

'I don't know. He had quite a lot of money in dollars, a big roll.'

Reeder scratched his chin thoughtfully, but made no comment, and the girl went on.

'I thought maybe there was something wrong at the bank, and I had an idea that he'd borrowed this money and was putting things right. And yet he wasn't very happy about it. He told me that he might have to go out of the country for a few months, and that if he did I wasn't to worry.'

'Was he a cheerful sort of fellow?'

'Very,' she said emphatically, 'until the past year, when property went down. He used to do quite a lot of buying and selling, and I think he made a lot of money before the slump came.'

'Had he any friends in London?'

She shook her head.

'None you know? You've not met any?' he insisted. 'No,' she said. 'There used to be a man who called here, but he was not a friend.' She hesitated. 'I don't know whether I'm doing him any harm by telling you all this, but Johnny is really a very good man, a man of the highest principles. Something has gone wrong with him in the past few months, but I haven't the slightest idea what it was. He has been having terrible fits of depression, and one night he told me that it was much better that his conscience should be at rest than that he should tide over his difficulties. He wrote a long statement, which I knew was intended for the bank. He sat up half one night writing, and then he must have changed his mind because in the morning, while we were at breakfast, he took it out of his pocket, reread it and put in the fire. I have a feeling, Mr Reeder, that he was not acting entirely on his own; that there was somebody behind him directing him.'

Reeder nodded.

'That is the feeling I have, Miss Reigate,' he

said, 'and if your brother is as you describe him, I think we shall learn a lot from him.'

'He has been under somebody's influence,' said the girl, 'and I am sure I know who that somebody was.'

She would say no more than this, though he pressed her.

'Can I send him food in prison?' she asked, and learned now for the first time about the bail and Reigate's mysterious disappearance. She did not know Polkley, and so far as she was aware her brother had no association with Newcastle.

'But he knows you, Mr Reeder,' she said surprisingly. 'He's mentioned you twice and once he told me that he thought of having a talk with you.'

'Dear me!' said Mr Reeder. 'I don't think he kept his promise. He has never been to my office—'

She shook her head.

'He wouldn't have come to your office. He knew your address in Brockley Road.' She gave the number, to his amazement. 'In fact, one night he went to your house, because afterwards he said that at the last moment his courage had failed him.'

'When was this?' asked Reeder.

'About a month ago,' she answered.

4

Mr Reeder went back to Brockley that night in a discontented frame of mind. Give him the end of the thread, and he would follow it through all its complicated entanglements. He would sit patiently, untying knots for days, for weeks, for months, even for years. But now he had not even the end of his thread. He had two isolated cases, distinct from one another, except that they were linked together by a similarity of method but, looking in all directions, he saw no daylight.

The quietude of Brockley Road was very soothing to him. From near at hand came the gentle whirr of traffic passing up and down the Lewisham High Road, the rumble of lorries and the shrill voices of boys calling the final editions of the evening newspapers.

In the serenity of his home Mr Reeder recuperated his dissipated energies. Here he could sit sometimes throughout the night, ambling through the dreams out of which his theories were constructed. Here he could put in order the vital little facts which so often meant the destruction of those enemies of society against whom he waged a ceaseless war.

He had very few visitors and practically no friends. In Brockley Road opinion was divided on his occupation. There was one school of thought that believed he was 'retired', and this was by far the largest section of public opinion, for everything about him suggested retirement from bygone and respectable activities.

No neighbour dropped in on him for a quiet smoke and a chat. He had been invited to sedate family parties during the festive season, but had declined. And the method of his refusal was responsible for the legend that he had once been in love and had suffered; for invariably his letter contained references to a painful anniversary which he wished to keep alone. It didn't matter what date was chosen for the party, Mr Reeder had invariably a painful anniversary which he wished to celebrate in solitude.

He sat at his large desk with a huge cup of tea and a large dish full of hot and succulent muffins before him, and went over and over every phase of these bank cases without securing a single inspiration which would lead him to that unknown force which was not only co-ordinating and organising a series of future frauds and robberies but had already robbed the banks of close on a million pounds.

Lewisham High Road at that hour was a busy thoroughfare, and nobody saw the extraordinary apparition until a taxi driver, swerving violently, missed him. It was the figure of a man in a dressing gown and pyjamas, darting from one side of the road to the other. His feet and his head were bare, and he ran with incredible speed up the hill and darted into Brockley Road. Nobody saw where he came from. A policeman made a grab at him as he passed, and missed him. In another second he was speeding along Brockley Road.

He hesitated before Mr Reeder's house, looked up at the lighted window of his study, then, dragging open the gate, flew up the stone steps. Mr Reeder heard the shouts, went to the window and looked out. He saw somebody run up the flagged pathway to the door, and immediately afterwards a motorcyclist speeding up the road ahead of a small crowd. The motorcyclist slowed before the door, and stopped for a second. At first Mr Reeder thought that the explosions he heard were the backfire of the machine. Then he saw the flame of the third and fourth shots. They came from the driver's hand, and instantly the motorcycle moved on, gathering speed, and went roaring out of his line of vision.

Reeder ran down the stairs and pulled open the door as a policeman came through the gate. A man was lying on the top step. He wore a red silk dressing gown and pyjamas.

They bore him into the passage, and Mr Reeder switched on all the lights. One glance at the white face told him the staggering story.

The policeman pushed back the crowd, shut the door and went down on his knees by the side of the prostrate figure.

'I'm afraid he's dead,' said Mr Reeder, as he unbuttoned the pyjama jacket with deft fingers and saw the ugliness of a violent dissolution.

'I think he was shot by the motorcyclist.'

'I saw him,' said the policeman breathlessly. 'He fired four shots.'

Reeder made another and more careful examination of the man. He judged his age to be about thirty. His hair was dark, almost raven black; he was clean-shaven, and a peculiar feature which Reeder noticed was that he had no eyebrows.

The policeman looked and frowned, put his hand in his pocket and took out his notebook. He examined something that was written inside and shook his head.

'I thought he might be that fellow they're looking for tonight.'

'Reigate?' asked Mr Reeder.

'No, it can't be him,' said the policeman. 'He was a fair man with bushy eyebrows.'

The dressing gown was new, the pyjamas were of the finest silk. They made a quick examination of the pockets and the policeman produced a sealed envelope.

'I think I ought to hand this to the inspector, sir–' he began.

Without a word Mr Reeder took it from his hand, and, to the constable's horror, broke the seal and took out the contents. They were fifty bills each for a hundred dollars.

'H'm!' said Mr Reeder.

Where had he come from? How had he appeared suddenly in the heart of the traffic? The next hour Mr Reeder spent making personal inquiries, without, however, finding a solution to the mystery.

A newsboy had seen him running on the

sidewalk, and thought he had come out of Malpas Road, a thorough fare which runs parallel with Brockley Road. A point-duty constable had seen him run along the middle of the road, dodging the traffic, and the driver of a delivery van was equally certain he had seen him on the opposite side of the road to that where he had been observed by the newspaper boy, running not up the hill but down. The motorcyclist seemed to have escaped observation altogether.

At ten o'clock that night the chief officers of Scotland Yard met in Reeder's room. The dead man's fingerprints had been sent to the Yard for inspection, but had not been identified. The only distinguishing feature of the body was a small strawberry mark below the left elbow.

The Chief Constable scratched his head in bewilderment.

'I've never had a case like this before. The local police have called at every house in the neighbourhood where this fellow might have come from, and nobody is missing. What do you make of it, Mr Reeder? You've had another look at the body, haven't you?'

Mr Reeder nodded. He had had that gruesome experience and had made a much more thorough examination than had been possible in the passage.

'And what do you think?'

Mr Reeder hesitated.

'I have sent a car for the young lady.'

'Which young lady?'

'Miss – er – Reigate, the sister of our young friend.'

He heard the ring of the bell and himself went down to open the door. It was the girl he had sent for. He took her into a small room on the ground floor.

'I'm going to ask you a question, Miss Reigate, which I'll be glad if you can answer. Had your brother any distinguishing marks on his body that you would be able to recognise?'

She nodded without hesitation.

'Yes,' she said, a little breathlessly. 'He had a small strawberry mark on his forearm, just below the elbow.'

'The left forearm?' asked Mr Reeder quickly.

'Yes, the left forearm. Why? Has he been found?'

'I'm afraid he has,' said Mr Reeder gently.

He told her his suspicion and left her with his housekeeper whilst he went up to explain to the men from the Yard just what he had discovered.

'It was very clear to me,' he said, 'that the hair had been dyed and the eyebrows shaved.'

'Reigate?' said the Chief Constable incredulously. 'If that's Reigate I'm a Dutchman. I've got a photograph of him. He's fair, almost a light blonde.'

'The hair is dyed, very cleverly and by an expert.' Reeder pointed to the dollar bills lying on the table. 'The money was part of the system, the disguise was part of the system. Did you notice anything about the clothes?'

'I noticed they smelt strongly of camphor,' said one of the detectives. 'I've just been remarking to the Chief Constable that it almost seems as if the pyjamas and dressing gown had been kept packed away from moths. My theory is that he must have had an outfit stowed away all ready for his getaway.'

Mr Reeder shook his head.

'Not exactly that,' he said; 'but the camphor smell is a very important clue. I can't tell you why, gentlemen, because I am naturally secretive.'

The body was identified beyond any question by the distressed and weeping girl. It was that of Jonathan Reigate, sometime

Assistant Manager of the Wembley branch of the London and Northern Banking Corporation. He had been killed by four shots fired from a .38 automatic pistol, and any three of the four shots would have been fatal. As for the motorcyclist, there was no one else who could identify him or give the least clue.

At nine o'clock the next morning Reeder, accompanied by a detective-sergeant, made a minute search of the Reigate flat. It was a small, comfortably furnished apartment consisting of four rooms, a kitchen and a bathroom.

Reigate had occupied the larger of the two bedrooms, and in one corner was a small roll-top writing desk which was locked when they arrived.

The dead man was evidently very methodical. The pigeon-holes were crammed with methodical memoranda, mainly dealing with the properties he had bought and sold. These the two men inspected item by item before they made a search of the drawers.

In the last drawer they found a small steel box which, after very considerable difficulty, they succeeded in opening. Inside were two insurance policies, a small memorandum book, in which apparently Reigate had kept a very full record of his family accounts and, in a small pay envelope, sealed down, they discovered two Yale keys. They were quite new and were fastened together by a flat steel ring. An inspection of these showed Reeder that they were intended for different locks, one being slightly larger than the other. There was no name on them and no indication whatever as to their purpose.

He examined the keys under a powerful magnifying glass, and the conclusion he reached was that probably they had never been used. At the bottom of the box, and almost overlooked because it lay under a black card that covered the bottom, he found a sheet of paper torn from a small notebook. Its contents were in a copperplate hand; certain words were underlined in red ink, carefully ruled. It consisted of a column of street names, and against each was a time. Mr Reeder observed that the times ranged from ten in the morning till four o'clock in the afternoon, and that the streets (he knew London very well) were side streets adjacent to main thoroughfares. Against certain of the times and places a colour was indicated: red, yellow, white, pink; but these had been struck out in pencil, and in the same medium the word 'yellow' had been written against all of them.

'What do you make of those, Mr Reeder?'

Reeder looked through the list again carefully.

'I rather imagine,' he said, 'that it's a list of rendezvous. At this place and at this time there was a car ready to pick him up. Originally it was intended to have four cars, but for some reason or other this was impracticable. I take it that the colour means a flower or a badge of some kind by which Reigate could distinguish the car that was picking him up.'

Later at Scotland Yard he elaborated his theory to an interested circle.

'What is clear now, if it wasn't clear before,' he said, 'is that there is an organisation working in England against the banks. It is more dangerous than I imagined, for obviously the man or men behind it will stop at nothing to save themselves if matters ever come to a pinch. They killed Reigate because they thought – and rightly – that he was coming to betray them.'

5

Mr Reeder claimed that he had a criminal mind. That night, in his spacious study at Brockley, he became a criminal. He organised bank robberies; he worked out systems of defalcations; he visualised all the difficulties that the brain of such an organisation would have to contend against. The principal problem was to get out of England men who were known and whose descriptions had been circulated as being wanted by the police. Every port and every airport was watched; there was a detective staff at every aerodrome; Ostend, Calais, Boulogne, Flushing, the Hook of Holland, Havre and Dieppe were staffed by keen observers. No Atlantic liner sailed but it carried an officer whose business it was to identify questionable passengers.

For hours Mr Reeder wallowed in his wickedness. Scheme succeeded scheme; possibility and probability were rubbed against one another and cancelled themselves out.

What was the organiser's chief difficulty? To avoid a close inspection of his protégés, and to keep them in a place where they would not be recognised.

The case of Reigate was a simple one. He was a man with a conscience, and though apparently he was heading for safety, that still, small voice of his had grown louder and he had decided to make a clean breast of everything. Having reached this decision, he had escaped from wherever he was confined and had made his way to Reeder's house – his sister had told the detective that the young man knew his address.

At midnight Mr Reeder rose from his desk, lit his thirtieth cigarette, and stood for a long time with his back to the fireplace, the cigarette drooping limply from his mouth, his head on one side like a cockatoo, and cogitated upon his criminal past.

He went to bed that night with a sense that he was groping through a fog towards a certain door, and that when that door was opened the extraordinary happenings of the past few months would be susceptible of a very simple explanation.

On the following morning Mr Reeder was in his office, and those who are not acquainted with his methods would have been amazed to find that he was engaged in reading a fairy story. He read it furtively, hiding it away in the drawer of his desk, whenever there was the slightest suggestion of somebody entering. He loved fairy stories about wonderful little ladies who appeared mysteriously out of nowhere, and rendered marvellous assistance to poor but beautiful daughters of woodcutters, transforming them with a wave of their wands into no less lovely princesses, and by a similar wave turned wicked men and women into trees and rabbits and black cats. There were so many men and women in the world whom he would have turned into trees and rabbits and black cats.

He was reading the latest of his finds *(Fairy Twinklefeet and the Twelve Genii)* when he heard a heavy cough outside his door and the confident rap of the commissionaire's knuckles. He put away the book, closed the drawer, and said:

'Come in.'

'Dr Carl Jansen, sir.'

Mr Reeder leaned back in his chair.

'Show him in, please,' he said.

Dr Jansen was tall, rather stout, very genial. He spoke with the slightest of foreign accents.

'May I sit, please?' He beamed and drew his chair up to the desk almost before Mr Reeder had murmured his invitation. 'It was in my mind to see you, Mr Reeder, to ask you to undertake a small commission for me, but I understand you are no longer private detective but official, eh?'

Reeder bowed. His fingertips were together. He was looking at the newcomer from under his shaggy brows.

'I am in a very peculiar position,' said Dr Jansen. 'I conduct here a small clinic for diseases of the 'eart, for various things. I am a generous man; I cannot 'elp it.' He waved an extravagant hand. 'I give, I lend, I do not ask for security, and I am – what is the word? – swindled. Now a great misfortune has come to me. I loaned a man a thousand pounds.' He leaned confidentially across the table. 'He has got into trouble – you have seen the case in the papers – Mr Hallaty, the banker.'

He waved his agitated hands again.

'He has gone out of the country without saying a word, without paying a penny, and now he writes to me to ask me for a prescription for the 'eart.'

Mr Reeder leaned back in his chair.

'He's written from where?' he asked.

'From 'Olland. I come from 'Olland; it is my 'ome.'

'Have you got the letter?'

The man fished out a pocketbook and from this extracted a sheet of notepaper. The moment Reeder saw it he recognised Hallaty's handwriting. It was very brief.

'DEAR DOCTOR,

I must have the prescription for my heart. I have lost it. I cannot give you my address. Will you please advertise it in the agony column of *The Times?*'

It was sighed 'H.'

If Dr Jansen could have looked under those shaggy eyebrows he would have seen Mr Reeder's eyes light up.

'May I keep this letter?' he asked.

The big man shrugged.

'Why, surely. I am glad that you should, because this gentleman seems to be in trouble with the police, and I do not want to be mixed up in it, except that I would like to get my thousand pounds. The prescription I will advertise because it is humanity.'

Dr Jansen took his departure after giving his address, which was a small flat in Pimlico. He was hardly out of the building before Mr Reeder had verified his name and his qualifications from a work of reference. The letter he carried to Scotland Yard and to the Chief Constable.

'Smell it,' he said.

The Chief sniffed.

'Camphor – and not exactly camphor. It's the same as we found in young Reigate's dressing gown. I've sent it down to the laboratory; they say it's camphorlactine, a very powerful disinfectant and antiseptic, sometimes used in cases of infectious diseases.'

He heard a smack as Mr Reeder's hands came together, and looked up in astonishment.

'Dear, dear me!' said Mr Reeder.

He almost purred the words.

When he got back to his office in Whitehall the commissionaire told him that a lady was waiting to see him. Mr Reeder frowned.

'All right, show her in,' he said.

He pushed up the most comfortable chair for her.

'Mr Reeder' – she spoke quickly and nervously – 'I have found a notebook of my brother's and the full amounts that he took–'

'I have those,' said Reeder. 'It is not a very large amount, certainly not such an amount as would have justified the trouble and pains they took to get him out on bail.'

'And in the notebook was this.' She put a little cutting on the table.

Mr Reeder adjusted his glasses and read:

'In your dire necessity write to the Brothers of Benevolence, 297 Lincoln's Inn Fields. Professional men who are short of money, and in urgent need of it will receive help without usury. Repayment spread over years. No security but our faith in you.'

Mr Reeder read it three times, his lips spelling the words; then he put the cutting down on the table.

'That is quite new to me,' he said, with a suggestion of shamefacedness which made the girl want to laugh. 'I'll have a search made of the newspapers and see how often this has appeared,' he said. 'Do you know when your brother applied for a loan?'

She shook her head.

'I remember the morning he cut it out. That was months ago. And then one night, when he had a friend here, I brought him in some coffee and I heard Mr Hallaty say something about his brotherhood—'

'Mr Hallaty?' Reeder almost squeaked the

words. 'Did your brother know Hallaty?'

She hesitated.

'Ye-es, he knew him. I told you there was a man who I thought had a bad influence on Johnny.'

He saw a faint flush come to her face, and realised how pretty a girl she was.

'I was introduced to him at the dance of the United Banks, but he was rather a difficult man to – to get rid of.'

Reeder's eye twinkled.

'Did you ever tell him to go away? It's a very rude but simple process.'

She smiled.

'Yes, I did once. He came home one night when my brother wasn't in, and he was so objectionable that I asked him not to come again. I don't know how he met my brother, but he often came to the flat, and the curious thing was that after the time I spoke of–'

'When he was unpleasant to you?'

She nodded.

'...He made no attempt to see me, apparently he was no longer interested.'

'Did you know Hallaty had disappeared after robbing the bank of a quarter of a million?'

She nodded.

'It very much upset Johnny; he couldn't talk about anything else. He was so nervous and worried, and I know he didn't sleep – I could hear him walking up and down in his room all night. He bought every edition of the papers to find out what had happened to Mr Hallaty.'

Mr Reeder sat for a long time, pinching his upper lip.

'Does anybody know you found this book and this cutting?'

To his surprise she answered in the affirmative.

'It was the caretaker of the flat. He was helping me to turn out one of the cupboards and he found it,' she said. 'In fact he brought it to me. I think it must have fallen out of one of my brother's pockets. He used to hang some of his clothes there.'

It was late in the afternoon when Mr Reeder turned into Lincoln's Inn Fields, found No. 297, and climbed to the fourth floor, where a small board affixed to the wall indicated the office of this most benevolent institution.

He knocked, and a voice asked who was there. It was a husky, foreign voice. Presently the door was unlocked and opened a few inches.

Reeder saw a man of sixty, his face blotched and swollen, his white hair spread untidily over his forehead. He was meanly dressed and not too clean.

'What you want?' he asked, in a thick, guttural voice.

'I've come to inquire about the Brotherhood–'

'You write, please.'

He tried to shut the door, but Mr Reeder's square-toed shoe was inside. He pushed the door open and went in. It was a disorderly little office, grimy and cheerless. Though the day was warm, a small gas fire burnt on the hearth. The dingy windows looked as if they had never been opened.

'Where do you keep all your vast wealth?' asked Mr Reeder pleasantly.

The old man blinked at him.

Reeder had evidence, apart from a bottle on the table, that this gentleman took a kindly interest in raw spirits. There was more than a suggestion that he slept in this foul room, for an old couch had the appearance of considerable use.

'You write here – we are agents. We are not to see callers.'

'May I ask whom I have the pleasure of addressing?'

The old man glowered at him.

'My name is Jones,' he said. 'That is for you sufficient.'

There were one or two objects in the room which interested Reeder. On the window sill was a small wooden stand containing three test tubes, and nearby half a dozen bottles of various sizes.

'You do a lot of writing?' said Reeder.

The little desk was covered with manuscript, and the man's grimy hands were smothered with ink stains.

'Yes, I do writing,' said Mr Jones sourly. 'We do much correspondence; we never see people who call. We are agents only.'

'For whom?' asked Reeder.

'For the Brotherhood. They live in France – in the south of France.'

He spoke quickly and glibly.

'They do not desire that their benevolence shall be publicised. All letters are answered secretly. They are very rich men. That is all I can tell you, mister.'

As he went down the stairs Mr Reeder was whistling softly to himself – and that was a practice in which he did not often indulge – although all his questions and all his cajoling had not produced the address of these Brothers of Benevolence, who lived in the south of France and did good by stealth.

It was too late for afternoon tea and too early to go home. Mr Reeder called a cab and drove back to Whitehall. He was crossing Trafalgar Square when he saw a car pass his, and had a glimpse of its occupant. Dr Jansen was looking the other way, his attention distracted by an accident which had overtaken a cyclist. Mr Reeder slid back the partition.

'Follow that car,' he said to the taxi driver, 'and keep it in sight. I will see that the police do not stop you.'

The car went leisurely through the Mall, up Birdcage Walk and, circling the war memorial, turned left into Belgravia. Reeder saw it stop before a pretentious-looking building, and told the cabman to drive on. Through the rear window he saw Dr Jansen alight and, when he was out of sight, stopped the cab, paid him off and walked slowly back.

He met a policeman, who recognised and saluted him.

'That building, sir? Oh, that's the Strangers Club. It used to be the Banbury Club, for hunting people, but it didn't pay, and then a foreign gentleman opened it as a club of some kind. I don't know what they are, but they have scientific lectures every week – they've got a wonderful hall downstairs, and I believe the cooking's very good.'

Now the Strangers Club was a stranger to Mr Reeder, and he was not unnaturally interested. He did not attempt to go in, but passed with a sidelong glance and saw a plate glass door and behind it a man in livery. The Strangers Club formed part of an island site. At the back some enterprising builder had erected a number of high buildings, tall, unlovely, their only claim to beauty being their simplicity. One of these was occupied by a dressmaking establishment. The second building had a more sedate appearance. Mr Reeder noted the chaste inscription on the little silver plate affixed to a plain door, and went on finally to circumnavigate the island, coming back to where he had started.

Jansen's car had disappeared. When he came again abreast with the club, the man in the hall was not in sight. He crossed the road and took a long and interested survey of the building, and when this was done, he again went round to the back. There was a pair of big gates in that building, which was indicated by a silver plate. He found a chauffeur cleaning his car, made a few inquiries, and went to his office not entirely satisfied, but with a pleasant feeling that he was on his way to making a great discovery.

6

Mr Reeder was a source of irritation to the staff of the Public Prosecutor's office. He kept irregular hours, he compelled attendants to remain on duty and very often held up the work of the cleaners.

What troubled him at the moment was the thought that in some way he had taken a wrong turning in the course of investigation, and that it might be straying into no man's land. For his own encouragement he had dispatched cables to various parts of the world, and sat down in his office to wait for replies.

He had hardly dipped again into his book of fairy tales, when the telephone rang.

'A very urgent message, Mr Reeder,' said the operator's precise voice. 'You are through to New Scotland Yard.'

There was a click. It was the Chief Constable speaking.

'We found Hallaty. Will you come over?'

In three minutes Mr Reeder was at Scotland Yard, and in the Chief Constable's office.

'Alive?' was the first question he asked.

The Chief Constable shook his head.

'No, dead.'

Mr Reeder heaved a long sigh.

'I was afraid of that. The trouble was that Hallaty was too clever. He wasn't in pyjamas, of course?'

The Chief Constable stared at him.

'That's curious you should say that. No, he was in a sort of uniform, looking like an elevator attendant.'

Late that afternoon a man riding a powerful motorcycle had passed at full speed in the direction between Colchester and Clacton. He had stopped to ask the way to Harwich, for apparently he had missed the road. After he had gone on, a light van had followed, taking the same direction as the motorcyclist. A labourer, working in the field, had heard a staccato rattle of shots, and had fallen into the same error as Mr Reeder had done on a previous occasion. He thought it was the sound of the motorcycle. He saw the van stop for a short time, and then move on. He thought no more of the matter until he made his way back to the road on his way home. It was then he saw lying half in the ditch and half on the verge the body of a stout man in a dark blue uniform. He was quite dead, and had been shot through the back. There was no sign of the motorcycle, though the wheel tracks were visible on the road, and had swayed off onto the verge. Thereafter they were lost.

Detectives, who were on the spot from Colchester within half an hour, searched the road and discovered pieces of broken glass, obviously portions of a smashed lamp. They found also a small satchel, evidently carried by the man; it was empty.

Hallaty's head had been completely shaved. The examination of the clothes showed neither the maker's name nor any clue by which they could be identified, but when the clothes were stripped, it was found that underneath he wore a suit of silk pyjamas, similar in texture to that which was worn by the unfortunate Reigate.

Mr Reeder made a rapid journey through Essex to the scene of the murder. He inspected the body and came back to London at midnight.

Again the Big Five sat in conference and Mr Reeder offered his views.

'Hallaty was too clever. They all suspected that he had a plan for double-crossing them. You will remember that he was a pilot and had a plane at the Axford Airport. When he went to take it out he found that it had been damaged and was unflyable. That was their precaution. Hallaty had to go either their way, or no way. Even in this eleventh hour he hoped to fool them. That empty case was probably full of loot. Harwich? Of course he went to Harwich. He had a trunk packed there and a passport. He had another at Brighton. You know you can get from Brighton to Boulogne on a day trip.'

'Did you know this?' asked the staggered Chief.

Mr Reeder looked guilty.

'I had an idea it might happen,' he said. 'The truth is, I have a criminal mind, Chief Constable. I put myself in their places and, having satisfied myself as to their class of mentality, I do just what they would do, and usually I am right. There isn't a cloakroom at any sea or air port in England that my agents have not very carefully searched, and Mr Hallaty's cases have been in my care for a fortnight.'

He was a very tired man, and welcomed the offer of the police squad car, which was to take him home. Tired as he was, however, he took greater precautions that night than he had taken for many years. With a detective he searched his house from basement to garret. He inspected the strip of back garden which was his very own, and even descended to the coal cellar, for he realised that he had made one false move that day – and that was to call at Lincoln's Inn Fields and interview the dirty little old man who had test tubes in his office.

He was sleeping heavily at six o'clock the next morning, when the telephone by the side of his bed woke him. He got up and to his surprise he heard and recognised the voice of Jean Reigate. It was weak and tremulous.

'Can I see you, Mr Reeder?... Soon... Something terrible has happened.'

Mr Reeder was now wide awake.

At his request the squad car had been held for him all night. It had remained parked outside his house not, as he explained, because he was afraid of dying, but because it would have been considerably inconvenient for everybody concerned if he did die that night.

He sat by the weary driver as the car sped through the empty streets and explained his system to a wholly uncomprehending and, if the truth be told, bored police officer.

'I think my weakness is a sense of the

dramatic,' he said. 'I like to keep all my secrets to the very last, and then reveal them as though it were with – um – a bang. You may think that weakness is contemptible in a police officer, or one who has the honour to associate in the most amateur fashion with police officers, but there it is. It's my method, and it pleases me.'

The driver felt it was necessary for him to offer some comment, and said: 'That was a very queer case.' And Mr Reeder, realising that his confidence if not rejected had been at least slighted, relapsed into silence for the remainder of the journey.

The caretaker had opened the main doors when Reeder arrived and was a little scandalised at this early morning call.

'I don't think the young lady is up yet, sir.'

'I assure you she is not only up, but dressed,' said Mr Reeder.

As he was being taken up in the lift, he remembered something.

'Are you the man who found the small book belonging to the late Mr Reigate?'

'Yes, sir,' said the man. 'Rather remarkable finding it. He had some press cutting about some brothers. I didn't rightly understand it.'

'Have you told anybody about finding the book?'

The man considered.

'Yes, sir, I did. A reporter from a paper came up here and asked me if there was any news. He was a very nice fellow. As a matter of fact, he gave me a pound.'

Mr Reeder shook his head.

'My friend, you have no knowledge of papers. If you had, you'd know that a reporter never gives you money for anything. And you told him about the book, I suppose?'

'As a matter of fact, I did, sir.'

'And the newspaper cutting?'

The janitor pleaded guilty to that also.

Jean Reigate opened the door to him. She was white and shaking, and even now she was trembling from head to foot. The previous night she had arrived home at eleven o'clock. She had been to see some relations of her stepmother and they had kept her too late. She opened the door with her key, went inside the flat and was reaching for the light switch, when somebody came out of the hall cupboard behind her. Before she could scream a hand was placed over her mouth and she was forcibly held. Somebody whispered to her that if she did not scream no harm would come to her, and almost on the point of collapse she allowed the men – there were two apparently – to blindfold her, and, when this was done, she heard the light turned on.

She was led into her sitting room and sat upon a chair. It was then that she became aware that a third man was in the flat. He was a foreigner and spoke with a harsh accent. Even though he whispered she noticed this, for there was an argument between two of the men.

Presently she felt somebody hold her by the arm and pull up the sleeve of her blouse, and immediately afterwards she felt a sharp pain in the forearm.

'This won't hurt you,' said the voice that had first spoken to her, and then somebody else said:

'Turn out the light.'

The man was still holding her arm and apparently sitting by her side.

'Keep quiet and don't get excited,' said the first man. 'Nobody is going to hurt you.'

She remembered very little after that. When she woke up she was lying on her bed, still fully dressed, and she was alone. The curtains and the blinds had been drawn up and she had a dim idea that as she woke she heard the door close softly. It was then about five o'clock. Her head was swimming, but not aching. She had a strange taste in her mouth and when she dragged herself to her feet, her legs gave way, and she had to support herself with a chair.

'Did you send for the police?'

'No,' she said. 'The first person I thought of was you. What have they done, Mr Reeder?'

He examined her arm. There were three separate punctures. Then he went in and looked at the bedroom. Two chairs had been drawn up by the side of the bed. The atmosphere was still thick with cigarette and cigar smoke. There were butts of a dozen smoked cigarettes on the hearth. But what interested Mr Reeder most was something the intruders had left behind. It was a fountain pen, and it had been overlooked, probably because the pen was the same colour as the table. He handled it gingerly, using a piece of paper, and carried it to the light. The pen was of a very popular make, but it offered a wonderful surface for fingerprints.

When he came back to the girl Mr Reeder's face was very grave.

'They've done you no harm at all. I don't think they had any intention to hurt you. I was the gentleman they were out for.'

'But how?' asked the bewildered girl.

Mr Reeder did not reply immediately. He got on the telephone and called up a doctor he knew.

'I don't think you will have any after-effects.'

'What did they give me?' she asked.

'Scapolamin. It's main effect was to make you speak the truth. Not,' said Mr Reeder hastily, 'that you ever speak anything but the truth, but rather it was to remove certain inhibitions. The questions they asked you were, I imagine, mainly about myself; what did you tell me, how much I knew. And I'm afraid' – he shook his head – 'I am very much afraid that you told them much more than is good for me.'

She looked at him with wide, disbelieving eyes.

'But who were they?'

Mr Reeder smiled.

'I know two of them. The third may, of course, be the most dangerous of the trio, but I really don't think he matters.'

That morning there was a swift raid on the premises at 297 Lincoln's Inn Fields, but the raiders arrived too late. They had to break open the door – the room was empty. Apparently there had been a considerable amount of destruction going on, for the gas fire had been dragged out of the hearth, and the original grate behind it was full of black paper. The test tubes had gone, and so had the manuscript which Mr Reeder had seen on the desk. Inquiries made on the premises produced very little in the way of information. Mr Jones had occupied his office for four years. He was believed to be a Swede, and he gave no trouble to anybody. Very few callers came. He paid his rent and his rates regularly and the only adverse criticism that was offered was that occasionally he used to sing in a strange language and in a stranger voice to the annoyance of the solicitor's clerks who occupied an office immediately below him.

Undoubtedly he drank. They found ten empty gin bottles in one cupboard and fourteen earthenware bottles in another.

After the raid Mr Reeder took counsel with himself, and examined his motives in the most candid of lights. He had, he realised, sufficient evidence to produce most of the effects which were desirable. He sent for a file dealing with the bank crimes that had been recorded in the past two years, and very carefully he went over the names of the men who had vanished, and with them considerable sums of money.

From his pocket he took the two keys which he had found in Reigate's pocket. If he could find the lock for these, the matter would be developed to its end. Mr Reeder was very anxious that he himself should fit these keys to the right locks, the more so since he had seen, as he thought, a very likely lock in the shop building immediately behind the Strangers Club.

He fought with himself for a long time. Starkly he arraigned his dramatic instincts before the bar of sane judgement, and in the end he condemned himself and sought an interview with the Chief Constable to detail his theories.

The Chief Constable had eaten something which had not agreed with him. It was a prosaic explanation for a fall of a great man, but he was at home, in the doctor's hands, and the Deputy Chief Constable occupied his chair.

It was unfortunate that Mr Reeder and the Deputy Chief Constable had never seen eye to eye, and that there was between them an antagonism which can only be understood by those fortunate people who have worked in or watched the work of a great government department.

190

The Deputy Chief was due for retirement. He had a grievance against the world, and every Superintendent and Chief Inspector at Scotland Yard had a grievance against him.

He was a little man, very bald, thin of face, and thinner of mind, and it was his boast that he belonged to the old school. It was so old that it had fallen down – if the truth be told.

When Mr Reeder had detailed his theories, 'My dear fellow,' said the Deputy Chief Constable, 'up to a point I am with you. But I will not accept – I have never accepted – the master criminal theory in any case with which I have been associated. There is a great temptation to fall for that romantic idea, but it doesn't work out. In the first place, there's no loyalty between criminals and therefore there can be no discipline, as we understand discipline. If the man is what you think, he could not command implicit obedience, and certainly in this country he could not find people to carry out his instructions without regard to their own safety. The other idea is, of course, fantastical. I happen to know all about the Strangers Club. It is extraordinarily well conducted and every Thursday there is a

191

series of lectures in the basement lecture hall: they have been given by some of the greatest scientists in this country. Dr Jansen has an international reputation—'

Mr Reeder was staring at him owlishly. In his soul there was a fierce, malignant joy.

'There can be no question or doubt that there is quite a lot in your theory,' the Deputy Chief Constable went on; 'but I could not advise action being taken until we have made very careful observations and there's no chance of our making a mistake. Personally, the fact that two men who were defaulting cashiers have been killed, suggests to me that there was a little gang operating in each case, and that somebody has tried to double-cross them.'

'And the silk pyjamas?' murmured Mr Reeder.

The Deputy Chief was not prepared to explain the silk pyjamas.

It seemed to Mr Reeder that the two Chief Inspectors, who were present at this interview, were not so completely happy about the matter as was their superior.

'As it is,' that gentleman went on (he was the type of man who always had an after-thought, and insisted upon expressing it), 'we may have got into very serious trouble in raiding the office of Mr Jones. I've been inquiring into the Benevolent Brotherhood, and they are most highly recommended by bishops and other important persons of the church. No, Mr Reeder, I don't think I can go any further in this matter in the lamentable absence of the Chief Constable and, anyhow, a day or two more or less isn't going to make any difference.'

'Does it occur to you,' asked Mr Reeder gently, 'that two men have been killed, there is quite a possibility of another seven going the way of all flesh?'

The Deputy smiled. That was all – he just smiled.

Outside, in the corridor, one of the Chief Inspectors overtook Mr Reeder.

'Of course he's all wrong,' he said, 'and I'm going to take the responsibility of covering whatever work you do.'

Mr Reeder made an appointment for the Chief Inspector to meet him after dinner, and alone he went back to the Strangers Club, carefully avoiding the front. There was nobody in sight and he moved carefully along the wall, until he came to a small door, inserted first one key and then the other. At the twist of the second the door opened noiselessly.

Mr Reeder dropped his head and listened. There was no sound. He had expected at least to hear a bell. Taking a torch from his trousers pocket, he sent a beam into the dark corridor. It was a little wider than he had expected and terminated, so far as he could see, with a flight of stairs which led up round a bend out of sight. On the left-hand side there was a wide door in the wall. He shone the torch upwards and saw a powerful light fixed to the ceiling, but there was no sign of a switch; presumably the light was operated from upstairs. He closed the door carefully, tried the second key on the bigger door, but this time without success.

At the appointed time he met Chief Inspector Dance and told him what he had discovered. They sat for over an hour in Mr Reeder's room, discussing plans. At nine o'clock the Inspector left, and Mr Reeder opened the safe in the office, took out a heavy Browning and loaded it with the greatest care. He pushed every cartridge into the chamber and out again, added a touch of oil here and there and finally, slipping a spare magazine into his waistcoat pocket, he pressed up the safety catch of the Browning and pushed the pistol behind the lapel of his tightly fitting coat.

The night commissionaire saw him go out, wearing one big yellow glove on his left hand and carrying the other. His hat was set at a jaunty angle and there was about him that liveliness which was only discernible in this very quiet man when trouble was in the offing. To his left wrist he had strapped a large watch, and as the hands pointed to twenty minutes to ten he walked almost jauntily up the steps of the Strangers Club, passed through the swing door and smiled genially at the porter.

That functionary was tall and broad-shouldered; he had a large round head and a wooden expression.

'Whom do you want?' he asked curtly.

Evidently the servants at the Strangers Club, though they might be handpicked for some qualities, were not chosen either for their good manners or their finesse.

'I would like to see Dr Jansen. He did me the honour to call at my office – my name is Reeder.'

7

For a perceptible moment of time he saw a light dawn and die in the dull eyes of the hall porter.

'Why, surely!' he said. 'I think the doctor is dining here tonight, Mr Reeder, and he'll be glad to see you.'

He went to a telephone and pressed a knob.

'It's Mr Reeder, doctor... Yeh? He just dropped in to see you.'

What the man at the other end of the 'phone said – and he said it at some length – it was impossible to overhear, but Reeder saw the man step back a little so that he could look through the glass doors into the street outside.

'No, that's all right, doctor,' he said. 'Mr Reeder is by himself. You haven't got a friend, Mr Reeder? Maybe you'd like to invite him in?'

Mr Reeder shook his head.

'I have no friend,' he said sadly. 'It's one of the tragedies of my life that I have never been able to make friends.'

The man was puzzled. Obviously he had heard a great deal of this redoubtable gentleman from the Public Prosecutor's office, and he was not quite sure of his ground. He gave Mr Reeder a long, scrutinising glance, in which any antagonism there might have been was swamped by genuine curiosity. It was almost as though he doubted the evidence of his eyes.

Evidently somebody called him urgently at the other end of the wire, for he turned suddenly.

'That's all right, doctor. I'll bring him right up. Will you leave your coat here?'

Mr Reeder regarded him with a pained expression.

'Thank you,' he said. 'I fear I might be cold.'

At the far end of the hall there was a door. The janitor opened it, switched on the light and disclosed a comfortable little elevator. Mr Reeder stepped in and turned so quickly that he might have gone in backwards. He had expected the porter to follow. Instead the man closed the door. There was a click and a gentle whirr and the lift shot upwards. It went up two storeys and then stopped, and the doors opened automatically – and there was Dr Jansen, very genial, very prosperous-looking in his evening dress and his heavy gold watch guard, with an outstretched hand like a leg of mutton.

'I am most pleased to meet you again, Mr Reeder. It is a great honour. You will follow me, sir?'

He went ahead, down a narrow passage, then, turning to the right, descended two flights of stairs, which, so far as Reeder could judge, brought him to the first floor. It was obvious that from the first floor which the elevator had passed there was no communication with this part of the building. It was almost unnecessary for the doctor to explain this.

He opened a door and disclosed a beautifully furnished room. It was long and narrow. A heavy pile carpet was laid over a rubber foundation, and the visitor had the sensation that he was walking on springs.

'My little sanctum,' said Dr Jansen. 'What do you drink, Mr Reeder?'

Mr Reeder looked round helplessly.

'Milk?' he suggested, and not a muscle of the big man's face moved.

'Why, yes, we can give you that even.'

Raising his voice:

'Send a glass of milk for Mr Reeder,' he

said. 'I have a microphonic telephone in my room. It saves much trouble,' he added. 'But you would maybe like me to shut it off?'

He turned a switch near the big Empire desk which stood in an alcove.

'Now you can talk and say just what you like, and nobody is going to listen to you. You will take your glove off, Mr Reeder?'

'I'm only staying a few minutes,' said Mr Reeder gravely. 'I wanted to see you about certain statements that have been made and which in some way suggest that this club is associated with a benevolent society run by an old gentleman called Jones.'

Jansen chuckled. Whatever else he was, he was a good actor.

'Why, 'ow strange!' he said. 'I know this Jones. In fact, I 'ave kept the old man alive. Is crazy, that benevolent society! But you know, Mr Reeder, it is quite genuine. Some people get a lot of money out of those poor men who live in the south of France.'

Mr Reeder inclined his head gravely.

'It has that appearance. In fact, I was speaking with the Chief Constable tonight. We were discussing whether there was anything sinister – if I may use that expression – about the society, and he took the view that it was quite genuine. I am

200

perfectly satisfied in my own mind that the brotherhood is responsible for giving quite a lot of money to people who felt an urgent need for it.'

Jansen was watching him, projecting his mind into Reeder's, taking his point of view – Mr Reeder knew it.

'The whole thing arose out of a discovery of an unfortunate young man named Reigate,' Mr Reeder continued. 'He was shot at my door and after his death there was found in a notebook an advertisement of this brotherhood. That, and one or two other curious circumstances... Oh, yes, I remember, two keys we found in his desk, gave the case a rather mysterious aspect.'

Mr Reeder was suffering under a great disadvantage. By a curious trick of mind he had entirely forgotten the excuse on which Jansen had called at the Public Prosecutor's office. Such a thing had happened once before, and he was as a man who was walking over a bridge from which one plank was missing.

'This man Hallaty now,' began Jansen, and in a flash the reason for the call was revealed. 'You remember, Mr Reeder, the man who owes me money, and who is in Holland.'

'He returned,' said Mr Reeder gravely. 'He

201

was found shot in Essex. Probably he had come back from the Hook of Holland to Harwich, and now—'

There was a tinkle of a bell and Dr Jansen opened a panel in the wall which hid a small service lift, and took out a glass of milk.

Mr Reeder sipped at it gently. He had a palate of extraordinary keenness, and would have detected instantly the presence in that harmless fluid of any quantity which was not so harmless, but the milk tasted like milk. He took a longer sip and put it down, and he thought he saw in the face of Dr Jansen just a hint of relief.

'And now, doctor, I am going to ask you a great favour. I am going to ask you to show me round your club, about which I have heard so much.'

The smile left the doctor's face.

'That I'm afraid I cannot do. In the first place, it is not my club, and in the second, it is one of the rules of this establishment, Mr Reeder, that there should be no intrusion on the privacy of members.'

'Of whom you have now many?'

'Six hundred and three.'

Mr Reeder nodded.

'I have seen the list,' he said. 'They are mainly honorary members who are admitted to the ground floor for your lectures. I've yet to have the satisfaction of seeing a list – um – of your members.'

Jansen looked at him thoughtfully.

'Why then,' he said, 'come along and meet them.' He walked past Mr Reeder, opened the door and stood aside for his guest to pass.

'Maybe you would like me to go first?' he said, with a smile, and Reeder knew that war had been declared, and followed him up the stairs. Again they were in the long corridor, and presently the doctor stood by the door of the lift, and pressed a bell. When the lift came up it was to all appearances the same elevator that he had seen before. It had the same black and white tiled floor, and yet Mr Reeder had a feeling that it was a little newer, a little cleaner than when he had seen it last.

As his foot touched the floor, he felt it give under him. Throwing the full weight upon his right leg, he sprang backwards. He heard something swish past his head. There was a crash where the short leaden club struck, and, recovering his balance, Reeder lashed out with his gloved hand. Dr Jansen went down like a log, no remarkable circumstance – for under Mr Reeder's glove was a knuckleduster.

For a moment he stood, automatic in hand, looking down at the dazed man at his feet. Jansen blinked up at him, and made a movement to rise.

'You can get up,' said Reeder; 'but you'll keep your hands away.'

Then all the lights went out.

The detective stepped back quickly, so quickly that he collided with somebody, who was behind him. Again he struck out, but this time missed. He was deafened by the bang of an explosion. He was so close to the pistol that the powder stung his cheek. Twice he fired in the direction of the flash and then he suddenly lost consciousness. He did not feel the blow that hit him, but went painlessly down into oblivion.

'Put on the lights now, Jansen. Has he hit anybody?'

The lights went up suddenly. The bullet-headed porter was looking stupidly at a wrist and arm that were red with blood.

A shorter edition of the porter came into view round the angle of the corridor, and looked at the senseless detective.

'Help me get him into the cubby, Jansen.'

Jansen only stopped to inspect the wound of the hall porter.

'There's nothing to it,' he said. 'Bind it up

with your handkerchief. It's just a scratch. Gee, you're lucky, Fred!'

He turned his attention to the senseless man. There was neither malice nor anger, but rather admiration in his glance.

'Help me get him into the cubby,' he said.

In reality he needed no help. He was a man of extraordinary strength. Stooping, he lifted the unconscious Reeder, dragged him through the passage into a little room, and dropped him into a chair.

'He's OK,' he said.

The little man, who had come from the passage, looked at the detective with an expression of amazement.

'Is that the bull?' he said incredulously.

Jansen nodded.

'That's the bull,' he said grimly. 'And don't laugh, Baldy. That guy's got more men in stir than any other fellow that ever broke from the pen.'

'He looks nuts to me,' grunted Baldy.

He had a shock of fair hair. Mr Reeder, who was listening intently, found himself wondering, in his inconsequent way, how he had earned his name.

'Feed him some water. Here, give it to me.' Jansen took a glass from the man's hand and threw it into the face of the drooping figure.

Mr Reeder opened his eyes and stared round. His glove had been pulled off. The knuckleduster had disappeared.

'I hand it to you, Reeder,' said Jansen amiably. 'If I'd not been all kinds of a sap, I'd have known you had that duster in your glove.'

He felt his jaw and grinned.

'Have a drink?'

He turned the leaves of a table and a nest of decanters rose.

'Brandy will do you no harm.'

He poured out a large portion and handed it to the detective; Mr Reeder sipped it.

Putting his hand to his head he felt a large egg-sized bump, but no abrasion.

'All right, Baldy. I'll ring for you.' Jansen dismissed his assistant. When he had gone: 'Let's get right down to cases. You're Reeder. Who am I?'

'Your name is Redsack,' said Reeder without hesitation. 'You are what I would describe as a fugitive from justice.'

Jansen nodded amiably.

'You're right first time,' he said. 'That Dutch accent wasn't bad though? Now how far have you got, Reeder? You and me are old-timers and hard-boiled. We'll talk it right out, just as we feel, and we're not going to get sour with each other. You went out for a prize and got a blank. There's only one way of treating blanks, Reeder – and that's the way you're going to be treated. Have some more brandy?'

'Thank you, I've had enough.'

'Maybe you'd like a cup of tea?'

Jansen was genuinely solicitous. He was not acting. He had pronounced the sentence of death upon the man who had come seeking his life, but he was entirely without animosity. Death was the natural and proper sequel to failure, because dead men cannot take the stand and testify to one's undoing.

'I think I would like a cup of tea.'

Jansen turned the switch and bellowed an order. Then switched it off again.

'You can't say you haven't met Jansen.' He grinned again.

Mr Reeder nodded and winced.

'No, I met him in Lincoln's Inn Fields – a very unpleasant old gentleman.'

'A clever old guy,' interrupted Redsack. 'In his way as clever as you. I picked him up when I came to England. He was doping then, and sleeping on the old Thames Embankment. He'd been so long away from home and he had no friends in England, I thought Jansen might be as good a name for me as for him, and he didn't care anyway. It's been a grand racket, Reeder; if I clear up tonight we'll go on for a year or two.

'I came to this country with ten thousand dollars. Part of it I brought on the boat, and part of it I snitched from a passenger's cabin. It was so long since I'd been in England that I didn't know how easy it was. You're all so damn law-abiding here that any big racket, if it looks good, would surely get past.'

He settled himself comfortably in his chair, but rose almost immediately to open the panel, and take out a cup of tea.

'You can drink that. If you like, I'll drink half of it. Say, these poisoners make me sick. You know what I got the dungeon for in Sing-Sing? It was for beating up a guy who'd poisoned his wife and mother-in-law. I just hated to see him around. He told them I was trying to escape and that he wouldn't stand by me. But that's ancient history, Mr Reeder. Drink your tea.'

Mr Reeder drank and put down the cup carefully.

'I wasn't a month in this country before I found a young bank clerk who'd been playing the races and snitching money from

208

the bank. He got tight and told me all about it, and I saw how easy it was to make big money; so I just organized him, and he got away with a hundred thousand dollars.'

He leaned forward and raised a warning finger.

'Don't say I didn't play fair with him, because I did. We shared fifty-fifty. The great thing was to hide him up for a month, and the next big thing was to get him away, and that was hard. I never realised before that England was surrounded by water, and that's where Jansen came in useful. I set him up in some rooms in Harley Street, but he was never entirely satisfactory, because we couldn't keep him sober. We had one or two narrow escapes with the invalids he was escorting across the Channel.' He chuckled as though it were a pleasant memory, and then with a deprecating smile: 'You know what it is, Reeder, when you and me have to depend on second-class people and not on ourselves. We're so near being sunk that a lifebelt doesn't mean a damned thing.'

'When did you start the nursing home for infectious diseases?'

Mr Redsack laughed uproariously and smacked his knee.

'Say, I wasn't sure whether you knew

about that. You're clever. You got it, did you? Why, that happened after one or two of these birds had tried to double-cross us. You see, what we did was to put this advertisement in every paper once a week. Naturally we had thousands of letters, but we waited till we got a man who could hand in the dough. You've got no idea how bank clerks don't know how to look after money! If he was just an ordinary five-cent man, we passed him on. But you'd be surprised at the number of big fellows – I once had an Assistant General Manager, who was so old that he couldn't be dishonest. But we got a good few real smarties; as soon as we picked on them, we'd tell them that, as a very special honour and on the recommendation of the Lord knows who, they'd been elected members of the Strangers Club. We got a whole range of private rooms. But naturally we didn't want any member to meet another member. We gave 'em good food, free tickets for the theatre. Just made them feel they were staying with Uncle John. How the hell they thought we did it on ten dollars a year I don't know. But I dare say you find, Reeder, that thieves are mean cusses.

'Once we got them here the benevolent brothers started their operations. I was the agent, and I had to make sure they were men you could trust. I'm not going to give you the long of it, but it was not easy to get the smarties to fall for this grand idea. Most men are thieves at heart, but the thing that scares them is: how am I going to get away without a lagging? They can get the stuff all right, but where is it going to be put? Where will they hide? How will they leave the country? We did everything for them; passports, transportation. Why, we even chartered a tug to get that guy who pulled down half a million from the Liverpool bank, from England to Belgium, and he didn't leave from Dover either. He went from London by water to Zeebrugge, and was carried aboard and ashore on a stretcher with so many bandages on his face that half the people who saw him land were crying before the ambulance took him on to Brussels. We made more than half a million bucks out of that, and he is living like a prince in Austrak.

'We give service, Reeder. That's the keynote of our organisation – service. We took 'em out of London in ambulances marked 'infectious diseases only'. Can you see any policeman with children of his own stopping them and inspecting the patients?

Why, you could smell that camphor dope before you saw the ambulance.

'You guessed right when you took an inspection of our nursing home at the back, and you guessed right when, after you had opened the door, you decided you wouldn't go in. We keep all our runaways snug in that home for a month. Sometimes two months, and no harm comes to them. They are out of the country as per contract. Service!'

He shook his head, and used the word lovingly.

'We picked 'em up from the bank, we brought 'em to London, we hid them and we got 'em out of the country, and never had a failure. Hallaty was yellow. In the first place, he didn't bring all the stuff to us; he cached nearly half of it at a small public house on the Essex road. Then he tried to get away and we naturally had to go after him. That kid Reigate, he got religious. We thought we had everything set, but he jumped out of the ambulance on his way to Gravesend, and naturally Baldy, his escort, had to stop him talking.

'I'm glad you didn't come in when you used that key. I shouldn't have had the pleasure of talking to you. We had a machine gun on you, and Baldy was all ready with his motorcycle to cover up the sound. But you didn't come in and, honestly, Reeder, I'm glad.'

He was very earnest. 'You're the kind of guy I wanted to meet.'

He shook his head, genuinely sad.

'I wish I could think of some other way out for you, but you're tied up to your graft, the same as I am to mine.'

Mr Reeder smiled with his eyes, and that was very rare in him.

'May I say not – um – as a matter of politeness, but in all sincerity, that if I have to go out at the hands of a desperado – if you'll forgive me using the word – I would prefer that it should be the best kind of desperado and an – um – artist.'

He paused.

'May I ask whether you plan to let the matter end in this interesting and complicated building, or have you a more spectacular method in your mind?'

Mr Redsack smiled.

'You're a classy talker, Reeder, and I could listen to you for hours. Naturally you would think that I'd be thinking of something bad for a fellow who's given me the worst sock in the jaw I've ever had in my life.' He touched his swollen cheek tenderly. 'But I've got no malice in me. I guess we'll try the grand old-time American operation. We'll take you for a ride. If you've got any particular place you'd prefer, why, I'm willing to oblige you, Mr Reeder, so long as it gives me a chance of getting back before daylight.'

Mr Reeder thought for a minute.

'I naturally would prefer Brockley, which has been, as it were, and to use an expression which will be familiar to you, Mr Redsack, my home town, but I realise that this highly populated suburb is not suitable for your purpose, and I suggest, respectfully, that one of the arterial roads out of London would suit both of us admirably.'

Redsack switched on his loudspeaker and gave an order.

He took from the belt under his waistcoat a large-sized automatic and examined it as carefully as Mr Reeder earlier in the evening had inspected his own lethal weapon.

'Let's go,' he said.

He led the way, opened the door again, and Mr Reeder passed through into the passage.

'Turn right!'

Mr Reeder followed his directions, and came to the blank end of the passage.

'There's a door there that'll open in a

minute,' said Redsack encouragingly.

They waited a few seconds. Nothing happened. Pushing past him, Redsack rapped on the wall and a narrow crack appeared in one corner. It opened wider and wider, and the door swung open.

'Say, what's the idea?' said Redsack loudly, and even as he spoke he whipped out his gun and fired twice.

It was a lucky day for Chief Inspector Dance. One bullet whipped off his hat; the second passed between his arm and his coat.

He fired back, but by this time Redsack was flying along the passage and had turned the corridor.

When they came up, halting gingerly to feel their way, there was nobody in sight. They heard the whirr of the lift, but whether it was going up or down they could not tell.

Then again the lights went out from some central control.

'Back to where we came,' said Dance.

They fled along the passage, through the door, down the steep flight of stairs. These turned sharply, and Mr Reeder saw what it was. They were out in the mews, but not quickly enough; as Dance fumbled with the lock, they heard two gates open with a crash, the pulsation of an engine and the roar of it as it shot past. By the time they were out in the mews the Strangers Club had lost its proprietor, janitor and chief attendant.

'Both keys worked,' Dance reported hastily. 'I gathered he'd got you and I advanced the time five minutes.'

He saw Mr Reeder rub his head.

'Hurt?' he asked anxiously.

'Only in my feelings,' said Mr Reeder.

They made a quick search of the garage and found the battered motorcycle on which Hallaty had tried to make his escape, and the big ambulance with its warning sign, which had assisted Redsack so vitally in his ingenious scheme.

'If the Deputy Chief had given me the sanction to raid this place, I'd have had enough men here to catch 'em,' growled Dance. 'Where is this nursing home, and which is the way in?'

It took a long time before they finally reached the secret suites where three panic-stricken 'patients' were waiting their discharge to that life of comfort which their depredations had earned for them.

8

Back at Scotland Yard, a chastened Deputy Chief Constable was anxious to do all that was possible to correct his error, for he had been on the 'phone to his sick chief, and what passed between them is not on record.

In the middle of the night a more careful search was made of the garage. Mr Reeder had seen a door which, he had imagined, led to a store. When the lights were turned on, the thickness of the doors revealed the character of this store. It was a steel-lined safe – it was empty. The accumulations of five years' hard work had gone. A barrage, immediately laid down about London, was established too late, and at five o'clock in the morning a tug left Greenwich and proceeded leisurely down the river, made its signal to Gravesend and passed out into the open sea.

The thing that came between Mr Redsack and his future appeared in the form of a smoky cloud on the horizon, and a grey hull. From one tiny mast broke a string of little flags. The Master of the tug reported to his chief passenger and charter party.

'A destroyer, sir,' he said.

'What does he say?' asked Redsack, interested in the nautical drama.

The Master consulted his signal book.

'"Heave to, I am searching you",' he read.

Redsack considered this.

'Suppose we don't?' he suggested.

'He'll sink us,' said the alarmed Master.

'Why shouldn't we let him come aboard?'

'That's OK with me,' said Redsack.

He turned to the tall janitor, yellow-faced and shivering in spite of his heavy overcoat. 'If I was sure they'd take me back to Sing-Sing, why, I wouldn't mind,' he said. 'Sing-Sing's kind of a lucky prison to me. But now I'm so damned English that it's Dartmoor or nothing, I guess. Or maybe they don't hang people at Dartmoor.'

He considered the problem as the destroyer came nearer and nearer, and then he went down to the little cabin and scribbled a note.

'DEAR MR REEDER,
I said last night it was you or me, and I guess it's me.'

He signed his name with a flourish, sat down on the hard sofa, took out a cigar. He heard the bump of a boat as it came alongside and an authoritative voice demanding particulars of the passengers.

Mr Redsack placed his cigar carefully into a little polished stove and shot himself.

The publishers hope that this book has given you enjoyable reading. Large Print Books are especially designed to be as easy to see and hold as possible. If you wish a complete list of our Large Print Books please ask at your local library or write directly to:

Oxford Large Print Books
Magna House, Long Preston,
Skipton, North Yorkshire.
BD23 4ND